TALES

from the
TEXAS TIMBERLANDS

This is a work of fiction. Names, characters, places and incidents either are products of the author's imagination or are used fictitiously. Any resemblance to actual events or locales or persons, living or dead, is entirely coincidental.

All Rights Reserved

Copyright © 2024 by J. Andrew Rice

No part of this book may be reproduced or transmitted, downloaded, distributed, reverse engineered, or stored in or introduced into any information storage and retrieval system, in any form or by any means, including photocopying and recording, whether electronic or mechanical, now known or hereinafter invented without permission in writing from the publisher.

Three Things, LLC
221 County Road 3014, Dayton, TX 77535

Visit our website at https://www.jandrewrice.com

E-book ISBN# 979-8-9893600-2-4
Print Book ISBN# 979-8-9893600-3-1

This book is dedicated to the storytellers in my life, including my daddy, Jakie A. Rice, Sr., my brother, Charlie Rice, my brother-in-law, Frankie Barnett, and other relatives and friends who have shared the mysteries and humor of life as we have journeyed together on this terrestrial ball. I learned a lot from them.

CONTENTS

The Businessman and the Cowboy 7

The Lonely, Strong One 23

A Vision and A Destiny 31

The Storekeeper 51

The Dairy Farmer 57

THE BUSINESSMAN AND THE COWBOY

It was roundup time. Cowboys, real and drugstore, would descend on the Colter farm like vultures after something dead. Excitement would fill the air for three days. Calculations would be made to see if all the cows had been gathered from the two thousand or more acres of briar-infested woods. Ten to twenty bony dogs would wander around the farm looking for a good place to rest or to find food while they waited for the next foray out into the brush and trees. Relatives would come and go trying to soak up some of the annual uniqueness of the occasion. Food would be plentiful.

Luke Colter was not as excited as many of the others. Nor was he bored. All he really was sure about was the fact that he and his brother, Matt, would be doing all the work that nobody else wanted to do. When the roundups first started, he had always wanted to ride a horse and gather the cows—it looked so important and prestigious. He got his chance a couple of times. Once he had to ride a small Shetland pony, which could have cared less about being ridden, especially in the woods. The next time he rode an old horse that would stop when a vine crossed its path. Neither time did he feel important, much less prestigious. But he had seen the other cowboys work when he rode with them. The good ones worked hard and seemed to understand cattle as if they were part bovine themselves. Luke never seemed to develop, or cared to develop, the knack of being a good cowboy. So, for the next three days, he and Matt would be fixing fences, opening gates, throwing and branding calves, riding up and down the woods pasture roads with their father in a car. Instead of horses, chaps, spurs, hats, ropes, and saddles, the tools of their trade would be cars, pliers, hammers, staples, crowbars, and come-alongs.

Billy Colter, Luke's father, got more excited than anyone. He hardly ever did any of the physical work but planned and supervised most of the roundup.

He was good at it, but many of the cowboys didn't understand him. They were primarily interested in working cows, and to some that meant rodeoing. Billy was interested in the money the cows would make for him, not how much fun he could have with them. He was more of a businessman than a cowboy.

Today, though, the roundup was still a week away. Billy, Luke, and Matt were working on the stock pens. Billy built them fifteen years ago, expanded them seven years later, and, after a number of roundups and other livestock-gathering activities, they were beginning to show their age.

"Okay, boys," Billy said as he looked at Luke and Matt, "we're going to lift this gate and re-nail these strap hinges. This wooden block will help hold the gate up but one of you will need to hold the end of the gate resting on the block to position it. The other one will nail, and I'll hold the hinge."

"I'll nail," Luke said. He volunteered because he had a lot of carpenter experience. He had held jobs in high school and college working on carpenter crews, where he had learned how to swing a hammer and make it effective. He hardly ever missed the head of the nail, and he knew how to hold the hammer by the end of the handle to get the most leverage.

"Okay, Matt, you pick up the end," Billy said.

Billy picked up the strap hinge and deftly put it between the post and the edge of the gate as Matt held the heavy wooden gate in place. Luke positioned the 16 common nail into the hinge strap and began to pound. His first strike sent it an inch into the wood. Two more made it close to being secure. One last blow would do it— and just before he hit the nail, Billy sneezed. The hammer glanced off the head of the nail and hit the strap hinge, which Billy held on its extreme end with his right hand.

Billy jumped back, grabbed his right hand with his left hand, bent down, and immediately exclaimed, "Woooooshiiiiiit, four hundred and forty fucking volts!!!"

Luke looked down at his father. He thought he had hit him with the hammer. "Daddy, are you alright?"

By that time, his father was shaking his hand. Matt let go of the gate and turned around, laughing as hard as he could. Luke was trying to contain his laughter after hearing the expletive. It was original and so much like his father. Most everything was black and white with Billy. If something hurt like hell, you described it in a manner that left no doubt about how it felt.

Billy looked up at both of them like he was ready to rip their heads off and then said, "You boys quit jacking around and let's get this gate up. You didn't hit me, Luke. The hammer hit that hinge. It vibrated like the titties on a New Orleans tassel twirler and stung the ever-living shit out of me."

Luke and Matt doubled over with laughter. It was more than they could take. They tried to stop, but it was tough. Then they saw their father start back toward the gate and knew it was time to go to work. Billy didn't say anything else to them, but the few moments of levity seemed to lift their spirits and the gate was in place twenty minutes later. The rest of the day was consumed with digging postholes, setting railroad ties for posts, and reinforcing the stock pen sides and chute.

The chute needed some special attention, especially after last year's roundup. Luke would never forget the show in the chute. Billy had bought a three-year-old, muley, Braford bull—a bovine with Brahma and Hereford genetics. At 1,800 pounds, he had the weight and strength of a Hereford bull but the temperament of a Brahma bull. He needed to be branded with the X 2 brand. He had another brand on his hip. The X 2 brand would be placed between his hip and his shoulder. In 1972, it was necessary in the East Texas woods to brand cattle, especially bulls. With their weight and muscle, they could easily get through weak places in fences, especially when cows on the other side of the fence were in heat. There were many times when people would let Luke, Matt, and his dad know that bulls and sometimes cows were in another pasture next to their property. The brand depicted the owner and most people around the area knew Billy's brand. The Colter men would run the wandering bovines back into their pasture and fix the fence, or the neighbor would pen them and let Billy know.

As Luke reminisced about the branding last year, he looked at the chute again. When the bull was first hit with the hot branding iron, he stood straight up on his hind legs bellowing loudly. He lost his footing and fell on his back. He then proceeded to kick the sides of the chute as he sought to get back up on his feet. He kicked out several thick cypress and oak boards. Posts were knocked down. There was some fear from the cowboys he would completely kick out the sides of the chute. His feet found some purchase, and he moved back and forth with indescribable strength and determination to stand up. Luke watched as the walls of the chute violently moved out and then in and then out again as the bull finally stood up. He was facing the exact opposite direction from where he entered. His eyes were bloodshot and primeval. He looked like a monster ready to kill anything in his way. He started head-butting the chute gate, bellowing all the while. All of the cowboys had moved away from the chute. Some had crawled up on the sides of the stock pens. They thought he was surely going to break out.

Then he quit bellowing and stood there breathing heavily, looking at the chute gate. Everything was quiet except for the sound of Billy's footsteps as he walked up close to the chute. He looked at the bull and saw that the X brand had burned the hide. Billy shouted for everyone to hear, "The X is good enough."

He opened the chute gate, and the bull moved out to the pasture. Nothing had been done to the chute since the previous year. The bull branding was always the last thing to happen at the roundup. Luke looked at the devastation and thought about the power it took to destroy the chute. That bull was a magnificent animal. He had survived, and throughout the last year he did his job in fine fashion. Even though Luke was off at college most of the time, he had seen the bull topping cows every time he was home. He even had a run-in with him one time when the bull got into the Colters' fenced-in yard. Luke opened the yard gate and proceeded to shoo him out. The bull didn't like Luke moving that close to him and started after him. Luke ran away and got through the back door of the house just before the bull could reach him. Luke smiled and shook his head at the memory of it. Then he started digging postholes and setting ties so they could rebuild the chute.

Billy's determination to make the stock pens strong and secure was motivated by brucellosis—or Bang's disease, in cowboy vernacular. A contagious, costly condition, it had plagued Texas cattle herds for years. A cow with Bang's would have spontaneous abortions and never give birth to any calves. If cows tested positive for it at sale barns, they had to be slaughtered, therefore causing the value of the cow to drop. A positive test meant the cow "Banged out." Billy wanted to get rid of the disease in his herd and was having all the cows and heifers tested, which meant the stock pens were going to be under a lot of stress.

There was one individual who always stood out at the roundup-Jim Colter, Luke's uncle. He was an elderly man in physical appearance but was only sixty in chronological age. He was sick and dying and seemed to know it. To Luke, Uncle Jim knew cows better than anyone else. He had seen him work many times. It was as if he and the cows were communicating telepathically. He never hurried. In fact, it irritated Luke's father sometimes when Uncle Jim seemed to be just fooling around. He probably had reason to be irritated. Much of Uncle Jim's life was spent procrastinating. He never appeared to be able to finish anything. His house was unfinished. He often talked of big projects but somehow never managed to start them. Livestock and just animals in general were different with him, though. Uncle Jim knew what, where, why, and how they would do something. When there was a job to do with animals, Uncle Jim was the best in getting it done.

Uncle Jim's wife, Etney, was as much a character as Uncle Jim. Like him, she had been married and divorced before they met. Uncle Jim had one daughter from his first marriage and Aunt Etney had two from hers. They never had children together but had been married thirty years. Aunt Etney's daughters called Uncle Jim their dad because he had raised them. Uncle Jim's daughter was older than they were, but he had raised her, too, since his first wife had left the two of them. These women, now grown, had a lot of respect for him.

Luke could tell Aunt Etney loved Jim. She was always doing things for him and was concerned about his health. She didn't mind him talking about doing things and never doing them. She never complained about unfinished projects. Until recently, they had lived in a shack with no indoor bathroom, a wood stove for heating and cooking, and no telephone service. She never complained.

Luke's mother liked Uncle Jim and Aunt Etney, but Luke had overheard her say they lived like people in "The Grapes of Wrath." He never understood that expression until he had to read the book by John Steinbeck in the tenth grade. Although the book was about Oklahoma people in California, Luke realized as he read it that he had seen people living like characters in "The Grapes of Wrath" all his life in East Texas. He had a much better living situation than his second cousins, who lived around Uncle Jim. They took baths in a portable steel washtub and often ate wild game they killed in the woods. Luke always liked to play with them. They would stay out in the woods, shoot birds, and cook them over an outdoor fire. They would use bacon as bait to coax crawfish out of a pond, then put pond water in a tin can and boil the crawfish in it to eat for dinner. But Luke never knew Uncle Jim's family was poor until he read Steinbeck's book.

Uncle Jim had never left this community. In contrast, Billy was the first one in his family to get a high school diploma. He then traveled throughout Texas and Louisiana doing geophysical work for the oil and gas industry and working as a surveyor for ten years. He met Luke's mother on his travels. They bought a farm not far from Uncle Jim and decided to settle there. Billy got a loan from the Farmers Home Administration and built a state-of-the-art farmhouse in 1952. Luke's mother had some pretty high standards when it came to living. He knew he had it better than most of his peer group, but his mother made sure he never bragged about it or ever had an air of superiority. He would get a tongue-lashing from her and, if bad behavior was serious enough, a whipping from Billy.

The best thing about Uncle Jim was his storytelling. Luke loved to sit on the porch at Uncle Jim's house and listen to him tell stories about his youth. He especially liked the one about the hog drives, when the Colters and Daniels would round up about a thousand hogs in the woods and drive them with horses and dogs to Lynchburg Crossing on what would eventually become the Houston Ship Channel. There, a buyer would put them on a boat and take them to Galveston to be slaughtered for market.

The hog roundup had to happen in January, February, or March, so that the hogs would not get too hot and would be in good shape for the sale. It was also best to slaughter the hogs in cold weather. Uncle Jim would regale them with stories about how the dogs would literally bring huge piney-wood rooters to bay by using speed and daring to dart in and out from the hogs' defenses, biting their ears, nose, and legs to the point where four dogs weighing around fifty pounds each had a four-hundred-pound boar submitting to them.

The dogs would bring the hog into the herd and move him and all the rest of the swine toward the objective. The men on horses with the dogs would ferret out the hogs from their hiding places in the brush, keeping the small bunches in a circle and then moving them to the larger herd. The hogs were collected in makeshift pens until the drive to Lynchburg. The hog roundup and drive would take around two weeks to complete.

One of Uncle Jim's most memorable stories was the one about Luke's dad and Uncle Jim's brother, Aubrey. One night he and Uncle Jim were hunting coons, and Aubrey got to bragging about the new backlit compass he brought along with him. Getting lost in the East Texas woods is very easy at night, even for experienced woodsmen. But Uncle Aubrey confidently boasted to Uncle Jim that he would never get lost with this fancy new compass. Uncle Jim just nodded. He was generally quiet unless he was telling a story. He also didn't have Uncle Aubrey's loud boisterous voice.

The hunt went well. They killed five coons. Uncle Jim would take the meat and Uncle Aubrey would sell the skins. Around midnight, they started to head home. The last landmark they had seen was an old logging road which they knew was just east of them. Uncle Aubrey looked at his backlit compass and headed off confidently in the direction of home. After they had walked about an hour, with Uncle Aubrey looking at the compass about every five minutes and growing increasingly frustrated, he finally stopped and turned to Uncle Jim.

"Shouldn't we have been at that logging road by now?" he queried Uncle Jim.

"Yep," Uncle Jim replied.

"Well, what the hell is going on? I'm heading east according to this goddamn compass, and we ain't there yet."

"Yep, well, I do know one thing. You see that tree right there with the broken top laying from the tree to the ground?"

"Yeah, so what?"

"Well, this is the third time we've passed it."

"Sonofabitch," yelled Uncle Aubrey, and he threw the compass as far into the woods as he could.

Uncle Jim then took a reckoning on the north star and headed east. They hit the logging road and got home around 1:30 am, a good hour after they would have without the compass.

The roundup was always on Labor Day weekend. Early Saturday morning, trucks and trailers with horses and dogs started arriving at the Colter ranch. Billy paid Jim to roundup his cattle. Jim paid one of the other cowboys, his son-in-law Jake. The rest of the cowboys were there at the invitation of Jim and Jake and were helping because they just liked to go "cow hunting." It was a phrase rarely understood by anyone outside of East Texas. Literally, cowboys had to hunt for cows in the woods, applying some good strategic thinking to find them, and then getting some help from the dogs in bringing them to the stock pens.

Luke remembered once being on a horse by himself looking for cattle. The woods were thick with briars and vines. He was able to make out a cow's eyes and horns through the thick brambles about twenty feet from him, right next to a tree. He was on the east side of the tree; the cow was on the north side. As he moved the horse toward the north to position himself to move the cow south, the cow moved to the west, right out of Luke's sight. He kept moving in a northwesterly direction, barely noticing the cow on the south side of the tree. She was heading east, where he had been located previously. They played that cat-and-mouse game around the tree for about twenty minutes, when finally, the cow broke through the woods to the north side of the tree in a dead run and left Luke behind, utterly exasperated. He never saw the cow again during that roundup.

As the cowboys rode off into the woods, Luke and Matt stayed close to the stock pens. They wouldn't be needed too much these first two days except to do some checking on the progress of rounding up the cattle. Some fences would be broken, and gates might need to be opened and closed. They would also drive cars and pickups into the woods to find out the progress of the search, checking to see if the cowboys needed anything and reporting back to Billy.

Billy couldn't help getting into the long slog of gathering the cows. He drove his 1962 Ford Falcon around checking on his cattle empire. He didn't want to ride a horse or drive a pickup truck. He was the antithesis of Jim. Billy had done plenty of horse riding in his younger life and pickup riding in the oil patch during his geophysical career. He thought horses were inefficient for work and pickup trucks rode too roughly. He mostly didn't want to spend the money on either one of them.

Luke watched as Billy made one of his forays into the woods. He was back in about an hour and drove up to where Luke was standing with Matt and a couple of the cowboys. Uncle Jim was sitting nearby under a pecan tree drinking coffee. Billy joined them.

"Well, it looks like Jake has about twenty cows coming this way from the northwest and Roy has a bunch coming from the south," Billy said. Billy always described locations in accordance with geographic directions. In fact, Luke would get instructions from Billy to take something from one place to another in the house. If Billy wanted the item in a particular place, he would say, for example, "put it on the north wall of my bedroom." Luke knew exactly where Jake and Roy were based on Billy's description. He had been taught well.

Billy continued, "I saw one of Jim's dogs at the intersection of the Mill Pond road and the main north-south road. He was wandering around there by himself."

There was a pause as everyone was patiently listening for Billy to say something else.

Luke thought he would be cute and take advantage of the pause. He said, "Well, what did you say to the dog?"

Everyone smiled except Billy. He lowered his eyes, gave Luke a smirk with a "you think you're a real smartass" look and said, "I told that bastard to get back to work." Then he walked away, leaving Matt and the two cowboys howling with laughter. Luke couldn't help but smile. His father had bested him with his own brand of humor.

Luke's mother, Wanda, and his older sister, Kathy, didn't participate much in the roundup except to provide lunch on Saturday and Monday. Some of the other cowboys' wives would bring food on those two days, too, but Wanda and Kathy did the bulk of the work. There was no Sunday lunch prepared by the Colter family, however. Wanda insisted that it was a day of worship and rest. She knew the necessity of rounding up the cattle and allowed Luke, Matt, and Billy to miss church that day, but that was the only reason they could skip it.

Neither Wanda nor Kathy did much physical labor on the ranch. Wanda would pitch in when Luke or Matt couldn't work, but Kathy never got into it. In fact, she just didn't like it. That role was primarily filled by her husband, Jeff. He enjoyed it, and he had money invested in the operation. Kathy liked to claim that she fed the hogs during a brief period when Billy had hogs. She did have a picture of the deed. Luke was too young to remember her doing it and believed the photo was staged. There was an ongoing argument on the veracity of that photo. Luke liked his sister, but now that he was older, he enjoyed teasing her. She was good-natured about it, but still didn't mess her hair up or get dirty on the farm. She mostly liked to stay in the house.

The big day had arrived. Saturday and Sunday were cattle gathering days. By late Sunday afternoon, there were eighty-two mama cows, eighty calves, and nine bulls in the holding pasture. The cowboys had also spotted six other cows with no calves. Two cows and one bull were not found, which meant only two percent of the mama cows were missing. Billy was satisfied. He declared that at 7:00 a.m. on Monday they would begin pushing the mama cows and calves into the stock pens.

From that point, the calves for sale would be separated from the rest of the herd, along with the older cows that were being culled and one bull who had been unmanageable for the last year. He was fighting the other bulls too much, had seriously hurt one of them and himself, and had knocked Billy down. That was the last straw. He was being sold. Billy made objective decisions about the cattle herd ninety-eight percent of the time. However, when the cows got out of line and started hurting other cows or people, they were gone. It didn't matter how productive they were.

Pushing the cows into the pens was not too difficult. By that point, the cows were used to the dogs and didn't want to mess with them. The dogs would circle the cows and bunch them up. One or two dogs would stay in the front of the bunch, guiding them in concert with the cowboys and horses. It reminded Luke of playing football. The cows were running the plays dictated to them by the cowboys, horses, and dogs, and the goal line was the entry to the pens.

Occasionally, a cow or a bull would break out of the bunch and run away. Two or three dogs nearest to them would take off after the recalcitrant bovine. This particular morning, it was the crazy bull Billy was going to sell. The dogs went after him. He was a reasonably big bull, around 1,600 pounds, with horns. He was also fast. Two cowboys rode after him and the dogs. The dogs turned him, and the cowboys, with their ropes in one hand and bridle in the other, got on each side of the bull. One dog had the bull by the nose and had bitten into his nostril. The bull was bellowing and shaking his head. The dog finally dropped off and came back to his ear. He jumped, bit the bull's ear, and held on. The bull was going nuts.

Roy Jackson, the cowboy nearest the dog yelled at him, "Heah, Buck! Get off that bull! Heah!"

Buck held on tight, and the bull started shaking his head while he ran. Luke watched, as he found the whole scene fascinating. The bull was bleeding from the ear. The other dogs were beginning to get more aggressive. Roy kept yelling at Buck. Finally, as if in slow motion and choreographed for the movies, the bull shook his head up and moved forward quickly as Buck let go of the ear and went into the air. He then landed on the tip of the bull's horn and cried loudly as it pierced his soft underbelly. He stayed briefly on the horn and was shaken off in the next move of the bull's massive head.

"Goddammit, Buck!" Roy shouted as he looked at the lifeless dog laying on the ground. He couldn't stop, though. The bull had to be penned now or they would never be able to pen him at this roundup. Roy took his rope as did the other cowboy and looped it over the bull's head. With two ropes on him they begin to struggle with him toward the stock pens. As the horses tightened the ropes, the bull would run and struggle in all directions to get slack. The trained horses would only allow it for a brief second and then move to reduce the slack. The dogs kept baying at the bull. Finally, he stopped. He was breathing hard. So were the horses and the cowboys. The dogs kept barking. Eventually the bull started walking and the cowboys pulled him into the big holding pen. He tried a feint or two to move away from his ultimate destination, but he didn't have the energy.

Luke was the closest one to Buck. He ran over to his now-still body. Luke had a deep admiration for any living creature that showed a passion for living and a mission in life. Buck was one of those creatures. The bull was one, also. They had met on the field of battle, both with a mission and neither wanting to bend to the will of the other. It was a magnificent show of courage, daring, and resolve. Before anyone else arrived, a tear rolled down his cheek. He quickly wiped it off and looked up to see his Uncle Jim on his horse, looking at Buck and then at him. An empathetic sadness was in Jim's eyes. Luke felt another tear roll down his cheek.

Jim said to Luke in a low, husky voice, "Buck was my best dog, Luke. Most of the good ones have short lives." Jim got down off his horse, picked up Buck, and put him behind the saddle. He rode toward his pickup truck and trailer. Luke watched Jim as he took Buck and put him gently in the bed of the pickup.

It was time to start loading calves and culled cattle. There were three holding pens. Two, one to the east and one to the west, funneled into the chute; the third one, on the north, was for holding special cases like the mean bull. He was in there at the moment. All the other cows and calves were in the chute holding pens. Luke always thought it was an interesting exercise, separating the cattle for sale from the ones who were not for sale. And this year there was the added dimension of brucellosis testing. Billy, with his business mind, wanted to get all the cattle for sale into the waiting sale-barn trailer. The sale barn was in Box Island, about forty miles away. It would take at least two, maybe three, trips there and back to get all of the bovines to the sale barn. In between trips, there would be brucellosis testing, worming, and branding. Billy would keep a few heifers to replace the culled cows.

It was Luke's job to operate the separation gates. He would sit on top of the chute and operate the gates as the cattle passed under him. The cattle would be run through the chute. Calves for sale would go into the trailer parked at the end of the chute. It could hold about thirty to thirty-five calves. The two separation gates would steer certain cattle into either one of the holding pens on either side of the chute. Today, the heifers to keep and brand would go to the east holding pen. The other cattle would go to the west and north holding pens.

Things had started off well, and the separation had gone smoothly, right up until the trailer was almost loaded. Then a cull cow with long horns got into the chute and was having a hard time navigating the chute because her horn spread was about six inches wider that the width of the chute. Her horns got tangled into the spaces between the boards, and she couldn't maneuver forward to the trailer. She stopped. There were about ten calves behind her to be loaded.

Luke watched from above the chute as two cowboys yelled at her several times and hit her with the hotshot, an electric prod powered by batteries. Luke had been hit with a hotshot once, and it had stung like nothing he had ever experienced. The cow still could not move. Then on trembling legs, she laid down in the chute. She was about nine years old. Luke thought she just couldn't take it anymore. Billy came up to the chute and looked at her. He looked at the calves behind her.

"She's sulling. Dammit!" Billy exclaimed, using a cowboy term for diseased or exhausted cows who would lay down and not get up until they felt better—or they would just die. He looked at the cow again. "Shit, I guess just run those calves over the top of her. We've got to get this trailer out of here!"

The cowboys pushing the calves used the hotshot on them until the lead one finally went over the top of the old cow and then the rest of the calves followed him into the trailer. The sale-barn driver closed the trailer gate. Billy counted the calves and wrote the number down in the notebook. He looked up at Luke.

Luke knew this situation was not good. Billy did not want to lose the $500 this cow would bring at the sale barn.

"Come down here, Luke," Billy said. As soon as Luke was down on the ground, Billy looked at him and said, "Go get your brother and the come-alongs. Tie them off to that pecan tree and pull that cow out of the chute. Loop a rope around her horns."

Luke got the come-alongs. He and Matt were bona fide experts with them. They had been stuck in mud so much feeding cows in the car that it was a regular occurrence for them to pull the car out of the mud. He and Billy had also lifted sulling cows with an A frame to try and get some life back in their legs.

He found Matt, and they rigged everything up to pull the cow out of the chute, moving her horns at an angle so that they would pass through the chute walls.

Meanwhile the branding, worming, and testing were proceeding in the holding pens and in the north end of the chute on the other side of the separation gates.

Luke began operating the come-along's lever. The chain to the tree and the rope on the cow were getting tighter. She was gradually moving forward but still would not get up. Then suddenly the cow's head fell down and her mouth went slack. Luke knew something was wrong. He stopped the pulling and went to look at the cow. Matt was standing beside him. He looked at Matt and said, "I think she's dead. Where's Daddy?"

Matt replied, "He went into the house with Jeff a few minutes ago."

"Go get him," Luke answered.

Luke grabbed the cow's horns and carefully moved her head. It was clear there was no life in her. Her tongue was hanging out of her mouth. Luke was upset. It was the second death of an animal he had witnessed today. He also knew Billy was going to be livid. He had experienced his daddy's wrath on several occasions in his life. Most of it centered around Luke's character development—things like his hair being too long and him just being plain lazy. Now that he was twenty, he understood better the reasoning behind Billy's reprimands. They had come to a compromise on his hair, and Luke had experienced the consequences of being lazy from other people, especially in college. He worked hard now, like Billy, and enjoyed the fruits of his labor. He appreciated his father's wisdom, listened to what he had to say, and then made up his own mind. Billy had personally expressed his pride in Luke, though mostly nonverbally.

The death of the cow was different, though. Billy would lose money. Billy and his siblings had grown up in poverty. Their father had died when Billy was four years old. They were raised by their mother in the 1920s and the early part of the Great Depression on a nearby farm. Billy would talk about how little money they had. Occasionally, they would sell fence posts or animals, and do work for other people when they could. However, they lived because of subsistence farming. It wasn't easy, but they made it work. On the few occasions they went to town, Billy watched his mother and other adults spend money.

Billy left home after he graduated from high school (eleven grades in those days) becoming the first high school graduate in his family. He immediately joined the Civilian Conservation Corps (CCC), and much was revealed to him about the wider world. He soon made it a mission to make as much money as he possibly could. He was passionate about it and sometimes let it override his relationships with his family. Wanda would then remind him there was more to life than making money. He begrudgingly listened to her but kept on his mission.

Luke knew that Billy loved him immensely. On the surface, it was hard to tell how Billy felt about things unless he was angry. Luke knew he would be angry about this dead cow and was preparing for an explosion. The loss of a cow that could potentially bring $300-$500 was not easy to stomach. Billy would roll it over in his mind for days.

Billy walked up next to Luke. Matt and Jeff were behind him. Billy looked at the dead cow. Jim rode his horse up close to the chute and looked in. "How did she die, Jim?" Billy asked.

"You broke her neck wrapping that rope around her horns—too much dead weight causing too much tension on her spine. Something had to give, and it wasn't the come-alongs," answered Jim.

"Well, shit, Jim," Billy shouted. "Why didn't you tell us?"

"You didn't ask," Jim replied as he turned the horse and rode off. Billy looked at the cow for a long time, kicking dirt and cussing. Then he looked at Luke, Matt, and Jeff, and said, "Okay, I'm going to salvage some money out of this cow. We're going to butcher her. Drag her out of the chute with the come-alongs all the way to the pecan tree. Then take the come-alongs off the trunk of the tree and tie it to the large limb on the north side. Hoist the cow up until you get her back feet off the ground. I'll get Jim to instruct you about how to butcher her." Billy then walked away from them to tend to some other roundup business in one of the holding pens.

Luke was aghast. He had never butchered a cow and had no idea what to do. He turned and looked at Matt and Jeff.

Jeff said, "I've butchered some hogs with my dad. I can probably do a cow. It shouldn't be that much different." Luke wryly thought, *Thanks, Jeff. That's just the reassurance I need!*

After they got the cow hoisted in the tree, Jim rode over and looked at her. Then he fixed his gaze on Luke specifically. "We're going to need five sharp large kitchen knives," he said. "I've got a Bowie knife, and I'll get Jake's Bowie knife."

Luke and Matt went into the house and got the knives. By the time they got back to the cow, Jeff and Jake had cut her belly open and were gutting her. They had built a makeshift table out of lumber to keep the organs and then gathered the rest of the entrails in a large bucket. Uncle Jim was going to take them home to feed his dogs.

Once the gutting was done, Jim showed Luke and Matt how to skin the cow, and they started to work. It was laborious, and Luke thought they would never finish. They had to get a stepladder to finish the shoulder area. During the skinning, Uncle Jim asked his grandson, Edwin, to start taking the organs into the house and putting them in the refrigerator or freezer.

The liver was first, and it was almost as big as Edwin. Luke caught a glimpse of the boy going up the back steps with the flat looking, fleshy meat spilling over his outstretched arms and drooping toward the ground. He knocked on the door. Kathy answered, and Edwin quickly said something to her. Kathy exhibited a horrified expression, let out a blood curdling scream, and yelled, "Get that thing away from me!" Then she ran back inside. Wanda came to the door, looked at Edwin, opened the door, and led him into the kitchen. Luke later learned that Edwin had politely told Kathy that her Pa wanted her to put the liver in the icebox. It was a moment Luke never let Kathy forget.

They finally finished the job. Butchering was indeed the best word to describe it in Luke's estimation. Although it certainly didn't look like the meat he saw in the grocery store. The muscle meat would be taken to a nearby locker plant, to be eaten by the Billy Colter family at a later time. The Jim Colter family would use the intestines and non-organ meats for dog food and eat the organ meats themselves. Jim also took the hide, from which he would fashion some leather straps. In the end, Billy had managed to realize some value from the cow. It was not a total loss.

Kathy would not eat meat for a year after this event. Luke had some of the meat later as steaks. Being a foraging-fed cow, its meat was very lean—but it was also stringy and tough, because the cow was so old. Billy was determined that the family would continue to eat it until it was gone. Wanda went to the locker plant a third time to pick up some hamburger meat, and the locker was empty. She told the proprietor about the empty locker, and he apologized profusely. He replaced it with some prime beef. Billy and Matt thanked God for his intervention. They had been saved from gastronomical hell.

For the past several years, Jim had let the younger cowboys gradually take over the work at Billy's family cattle roundups. Physically, he was unable to stay in the saddle long enough and withstand all the other rigor. His presence was known, however, by every person and even the cattle. The bull that killed Buck had been resting and was definitely energized. The trouble began when the bull would not go into the chute holding pen. The better cowboys on their horses tried to push him in, but each time he balked, turned, and ran back through them. On the third try, he gored a horse and broke the ankle of one of the good cowboys.

Next, some of the drugstore types brought out their ropes. Luke wasn't a good cowboy, but he knew that was stupid. One drugstore roped the bull around the neck, and that's when everything came apart. The bull started fighting it and pulled the rope off the cowboy's saddle horn, charged the horse, and gored it. The drugstore jumped off and headed for the fence. The bull barely missed him as he clambered to the top.

Luke hardly heard his Uncle Jim when he told him to go get his horse. Luke sensed that things were critical when Uncle Jim got into the act. Those guys had been working with that bull for an hour, and two horses and one man were hurt. When Luke brought the horse to Uncle Jim, the old man spat out his tobacco chew. Things were pretty serious when Uncle Jim got rid of his chew. In fact, he could only remember one other time when he had seen him without a chew, and that was at his mother's—Luke's grandmother's—funeral.

When Uncle Jim got in the saddle, he told the other cowboys to let him into the pen. The gate opened and the bull ran to the far corner, snorting and shaking his head. His ears were almost gone. The dogs had chewed them in the woods and the holding pasture trying to persuade him to bunch up with the cows. A long thread of saliva was coming from his mouth. He lowered his head and looked at Uncle Jim. He began to paw the ground with his right front foot. Luke had never seen a bull as mad as that one. His whole body was shaking like he would explode in the next second.

Uncle Jim and the bull looked at each other from different corners of the pen like two boxers waiting for the bell. They continued doing it for what seemed to be an eternity. Then Uncle Jim started his horse in a walk toward the bull, who continued to paw and shake. Uncle Jim gradually got closer. Then the bull charged. Uncle Jim stopped the horse. The bull feinted at the horse and pulled back. Uncle Jim started his horse again. The bull feinted. Uncle Jim stopped the horse. The bull stopped. Uncle Jim started his horse. It continued like that until the bull was near the holding pen. Luke noticed the bull wasn't shaking as much, and the saliva was not pouring out of his mouth. It was as if he had been given a tranquilizer.

The bull made a feint toward the horse and then ran into the chute holding pen. Uncle Jim had gradually cornered him so that it was the only place he could go. The whole affair lasted fifteen minutes. It was the best cowboying Luke had ever seen. Uncle Jim had coaxed that bull into the chute holding pen in the same patient, unhurried, caring manner a mother would use to encourage her scared child.

The bull and five cows were the last ones to be loaded and taken to the sale barn. The culled cows included those testing positive for brucellosis. All the branding of heifers and bulls to add to the herd had been completed, along with the annual worming. It was around four o'clock on Labor Day, and the roundup was over. Dogs and horses were gathered up and loaded into trucks and trailers. Luke and Matt picked up all the tools and appurtenances and put them in the barn.

While he was working, Luke stopped and watched Billy and Jim conversing with one another. Jim had a wry smile on his face and a twinkle in his eye, and Billy was laughing heartily. He thought how they made a good pair managing these entire three days of the cattle business. Billy, with his business instinct, saw a gross income of around $15,000 before anything even got started, but he needed someone to protect his assets and account for every animal without losing too many. His brother, Jim, came through for him, just the same way he had for so many years. These two men, survivors of family upheaval, the Great Depression, suffocating poverty, and the crises of World War II, were still gloriously alive. Luke couldn't help but smile as he watched the brothers shake hands and go their separate ways.

THE LONELY, STRONG ONE

Matthew Brunson knew he was headed for trouble. The old woman had been nothing but a source of disruption ever since he approved the government grant to fix her house. Why did all of those old people come to him when they had problems? Early that morning she had walked blindly into his office, pointed to a framed, needlepoint picture, and said, "Mr. Brunson it's not working--oh heavens, that's not it--I'm confused." Then she walked toward the door and screamed, "I--I--I just don't know what I'm doing. Help me, Mr. Brunson, please come to my house." There was no way he could refuse. He told her that she needed to go home, and he would be there in about fifteen minutes.

It was the end of September 1978. A lot of changes were taking place in the world, most notably the Camp David accords, where visions of Middle East peace danced in the heads of everyone. Matthew, in his twenty-fifth year of living, was excited to be working for the City of Buttermilk Junction, Texas. He was getting his graduate degree in Public Administration and had been given a job in the City's Community Development Department. He looked forward to contributing to the revitalization of the city of 15,000 people. It had grown quickly after World War II but had seen some white flight into other areas near Buttermilk Junction. Black people had seen a lot of opportunity to work in the numerous petrochemical plants and refineries located within a short distance of the city, especially after federal equal employment opportunity laws were enacted in the 1960s. However, some Black families had been in Buttermilk Junction since it had been a farming community, well before World War II began. The old woman visiting Matthew was a long-time resident of Buttermilk Junction. She was Black.

As a white man, Matthew had limited experience in relationships with Black folks. He had grown up in a mostly rural, white community in East Texas. His school had integrated when he was thirteen. In a school of five hundred students, grades one through twelve, there were only about twenty Black students in the entire student population. Then he went to a private university in Texas, where the percentage of Black students was even lower than in his home community. After he graduated from college with a Bachelor of Arts degree, he taught ninth-grade math in Buttermilk Junction so he could work on his graduate degree. Given his past experience, he was surprised when the percentage of Black students in his classes alone came to fifty percent.

He had been told by one of his former teachers to be a strict, mean son-of-a-bitch with all his students—at least for the first six weeks. He put that advice into practice and was rewarded with some very intimidated kids. However, a few kids challenged his intimidation tactics, especially the boys. Matthew had been an athlete and knew he could take on any of his male students, but he didn't want to do it. He really wanted to understand them and motivate them. After the first twelve weeks of school, a kid named Harold Reed came into his special education math class and didn't bring his book—a cardinal rule violation for Matthew's classes.

Matthew asked, "Harold, where's your book?" as Harold walked past him.

Harold didn't answer and sat at his desk.

"Harold, where is your book?" Matthew asked again.

Harold answered, "In my locker."

"Go get it."

"I ain't gonna git it."

"Yes, you are. Get up and go get it."

"Nope, I don't have to do what any whitey wants me to do."

It was a first for Matthew. He breathed deeply and vowed not to lose his temper. He responded with emphasis, "Harold, go get your book, now."

Harold shook his head.

"Then you need to go see Mr. Jackson."

"All right with me." And Harold got up to go see Assistant Principal Eddie Jackson. Even Matthew, who wasn't easily intimidated, was intimidated by Eddie Jackson. He was six feet four inches tall, fit, and covered with muscle sinew. He reminded Matthew of professional basketball players like Bill Russell of the Boston Celtics or Julius Irving of the Philadelphia 76ers. Matthew had never sent a kid to him, although Mr. Jackson had told the teachers to feel free to send their disciplinary problems to him if they had no way to handle the situation.

After class, Matthew was sitting at his desk during his off period when Mr. Jackson came into his classroom with Harold. Mr. Jackson always had a serious look on his face, with what seemed like a permanent furrow between his eyebrows. The whites of his eyes stood out prominently against his black skin and they always seemed to be a bit bloodshot. He was looking downright scary that day, and Matthew was bracing for the worst.

Mr. Jackson drilled his red, bloodshot eyes into Matthew and said, "Mr. Brunson, I need to see you with Mr. Reed in your storage room right now."

Matthew said, "Yes, sir." He opened the storage room door and walked in behind Mr. Jackson and Harold. He could feel his adrenaline kicking in.

The storage room was quite large. It had a table and chairs, filing cabinets and spare desks. Matthew only used the file cabinets. He shared the room with Mr. Sizemore, who almost exclusively used it for paddling students. Matthew had just witnessed a multi-paddling this morning. Sizemore had completely lost control of his classes, which resulted in frequent paddling and a lot of name-calling. The Black kids would jive down the hall and when they came by Sizemore's class, chanting "Disco Sizemo." Matthew thought it was funny. Mr. Sizemore did not.

Matthew stood at the table and faced Mr. Jackson and Harold. Harold was to his right and Mr. Jackson to his left spoke in a highly irritated voice and said, "Mr. Brunson, Mr. Reed has told me that he does not want to bring his book to class. Is that right?"

"Yes, sir, that's what he told me."

Mr. Jackson took his gaze off Matthew and stepped toward Harold. Looking down at him, he said in a strident, baritone voice, "Now you listen to me, you little ungrateful son-of-a-bitch, when Mr. Brunson says to bring your book to class, you do it. We're not going to have any of that goddamn shit around this school. You are here to learn what is in that book. Now you're going to take five from Mr. Brunson or you're going to jail. Which do you want to do?"

Harold kept looking down and said, "Go to jail."

Jackson grabbed Harold by the arm and was dragging him to the door yelling, "We're going right now."

All the air left the room. Matthew stood there in awe of what had happened. He finally stopped holding his breath and tried to process what he was thinking. Did Jackson actually turn the tables on what he thought was going to be a lecture on how a white teacher should treat a Black student? He walked back to his classroom with lots of questions.

Later that afternoon, after school was over, Mr. Jackson brought Harold back to his classroom. Jackson was in a much more subdued mood and once again asked Matthew to meet with him and Harold in the storage room.

"Mr. Brunson," Jackson said, "Mr. Reed has changed his mind about going to jail. He wants to take five from you instead. He will also be bringing his book to class." Jackson picked up Sizemore's paddle and handed to Matthew.

"Now, Reed, put your hands on that table and bend over." Jackson emphasized.

Matthew was caught. He had never hit a kid in his life. However, the discipline and its enforcement had been designed by Jackson, and he and Harold knew it. Matthew walked slowly over to Harold's left side and proceeded to strike him on the butt with the modified wooden baseball bat. After three, Harold was wincing. Matthew stopped. He said, "I think that's enough."

"There you go, Harold," Jackson said, "Mr. Brunson is going easy on you. You make sure you bring that book to class. Now go catch your bus."

Jackson looked tired as he sat there on the edge of the table and watched Harold go out the door. Then he said to Matthew in a sad, advisory sort of voice, "You must understand what we're doing here is dealing with kids who have very little if any supervision at home. I know Harold and where he lives. He got up this morning, had no breakfast, got himself ready to go to school and came to your class. If he does something wrong, his daddy whips him five times as much over small stuff as you did over his education. What we have in schools like ours is something like controlled anarchy. It would be nice for us to try and counsel these kids into good and productive behavior. But we don't have the time and the resources, and most of them don't understand anything about discipline except physical punishment for wrong behavior. That's why I had to speak to him as I did and why you had to paddle him. That's mild for what his real life is going to be like as he grows up. But I'm hoping that you will have that small influence on him which will keep him from living a life of crime, in and out of prison."

Jackson left the room. Matthew had never forgotten that day.

The old woman's name was Martha Green. At the age of eighty-nine, she was ninety percent blind, partially senile, crafty, strong-willed, and smart. She was an enigma. As a white man, Matthew had always marveled at these old Black women. Mrs. Green was the epitome of these tough survivors. How she had lived eighty-nine years was beyond him. Being Black during her early years had to have been excruciatingly hard. Racism had been the status quo. Even now, in the 1970s, it still made a powerful difference in a lot of lives, and not in a good way. He had heard that some poor Black women had traditionally been mistreated by their husbands or had been left to fend for themselves. She was no exception.

When Matthew arrived, Mrs. Green was already waiting for him at the door. She unlocked the two deadbolt locks on the door, the doorknob lock. and then let him in. As they walked down the hallway, she explained what had happened, but it didn't make any sense. Before they reached the next room, she repeated the same phrase he had heard since work had started on her house, "I--I--I never been so sorry I did something in my whole life. This has been a heartache to me. It's--it's just made me sick." Matthew was teetering on the edge of thinking the same thing about himself. Well, why not? Didn't he deserve at least a little more appreciation for his efforts?

Entering the second room, he immediately saw the problem. An electrical outlet had been totally dismantled by someone who knew what he or she was doing. There was also a burned place that snaked across the carpet for about three feet. From Mrs. Green's ongoing monologue, he began to fit the pieces together. She had plugged an electric heater into an extension cord that had been connected to the outlet. The extension cord was too small to carry the electrical load demanded by the heater and had burned to a crisp when the heater was turned on. A neighbor had called the fire department, and some firefighter had dismantled the outlet.

"Now what are you going to do about this, Mr. Brunson?" she asked. She's being crafty again, Matthew thought. She knows perfectly well that this was her fault and that it was nothing that needed to be corrected by the contractor's warranty. For the fifteenth time in the last three months, he bundled his nerves and prepared his statement. "Mrs. Green, there is nothing I can do. You caused this by plugging this heater into a too small extension cord. The damage to your electrical outlet cannot be repaired under the contractor's warranty. "

Her near-blind eyes focused on him with a resigned look. "Well, I figured as much." Matthew was surprised. She was not the kind that gave up without a fight.

"Now, Mr. Brunson, let me show you something else." She led Matthew down the hall and through the kitchen, out the back door, and into the yard. She pointed to a depression in the ground.

"Now, do you see that?" she asked.

"Yes, ma'am," Matthew replied.

"Now, Mr. Brunson, that plumber just didn't do his job. He just didn't do it. This line leaks and all that sewage gets in this yard."

This was not a new complaint. Matthew had his doubts about whether or not the plumber had done a first-class job, but there was no way he could prove it unless he dug up the line himself. In any case, he had never seen it leak,

"Mrs. Green," he answered, "I don't see where this is causing any problems.

Why do you want it fixed again?"

"Mr. Brunson, I'll be ninety years old on July 29th this year......"

He caught her in mid-sentence before he could stop himself "Mrs. Green, that's my birthday, too," he said.

She hesitated a minute and looked at him skeptically. "Is that right?" she replied, "Well, how 's your mother?"

"She's just fine," Matthew answered, although he couldn't understand the reason for the question.

"Are you married?" she asked.

"Yes, ma'am"

"How's your wife?"

"She's fine."

"How many children do you have?" she queried.

"We don't have any."

"Well, when are you going to get some? "

"I really don't know, Mrs. Green,"

She laughed and said, "I just can't believe we have the same birthday. You know, Mr. Brunson, I just believe in loving everybody. I believe that's what the Lord wants us to do."

"I believe so, too," Matthew agreed,

"I have some pamphlets I want you to read, Mr. Brunson. I got them at church. They tell people about how they should love one another,"

She continued with the story about the pamphlets and then talked about how she liked to treat people and how she wanted to be treated. She gave advice and carried on an amiable conversation with him for about fifteen minutes.

Matthew knew he had to be going. He had work to do. He edged toward the gate as Mrs. Green followed. He finally gave her his farewell, "take care of yourself" and walked out the gate. The so-called problem with the house had not been mentioned again. She didn't give him the pamphlets.

As Matthew walked toward his car and sat down in the driver's seat, he thought of Harold Reed, Eddie Jackson, and Martha Green. All of them had taught him something. He knew his life had been substantially better growing up than their lives. He had been given a lot more opportunities and privilege because he was white. He now knew the long struggle Black people and their ancestors endured to just survive oppression and the mysteries of life. He knew it had been easier for him. They really didn't want much from him except his respect. They just needed to know that they were equal to him… and for him to acknowledge something like sharing the same birthday.

As he looked through the windshield, the old woman climbed the steps to the front porch, Matthew understood that he had not been summoned to see about the physical problems of the house. He had been called to cure a bout of loneliness and frustration and had received the sought-after appreciation for his efforts.

A VISION AND A DESTINY

"Well, Kenneth Howell," exclaimed the kindly old man in the wheelchair, "you are a sight for sore eyes. I've been needing a little company, and you are just the person I need to talk to!" He was grinning from ear to ear.

"Hi, Mr. Wood," I replied, "I need to talk to you, also. Although my attitude right now is not as cheery as yours,"

He laughed., "Let's see what we can do about it. Come on into this house."

Lew Wood had been a fixture in Oakdale, Texas, for about as long as anyone could remember. He was the first person I wanted to see when I moved back to Oakdale after college.

I moved back to Oakdale, the community where I was raised, because I could not see much of a future in the place where I had landed four years earlier. I got my master's degree in public administration and worked in local government during that time. Granted, there were other opportunities in that town, but superficial, not life-changing, and without soul. I wanted to make a difference. My psyche was just not one for sitting around making small talk and waiting for something to happen.

My community needed me. They needed someone to care about them, to teach them, to live and die with them. I had obtained a good education and some skills I thought could help bring changes that would make all of us better people. I was confident I could do it with the beautiful and talented woman I met in college and soon married. We would establish ourselves in Oakdale, raise our children, and find a way to be instruments of the American way.

Today, though, I just kept finding myself thinking: *Where is Norman Rockwell when you need him?* Those pictures of America I saw in my mind reflected my community in some respects, but they also hid the unmitigated ignorance and fear, especially prevalent in so many parts of rural Texas. Why was I discouraged?

Time after time I had a vision about the progress that could be made in community development for Oakdale and the surrounding areas, but only incremental change was evident.

For instance, it was clear to me and many other people that because we lived in a geographically flat area, there was a problem with drainage. With an average annual rainfall of fifty inches per year, water just stayed in place. Four-wheel drive vehicles were prolific but even that amenity didn't preclude getting your vehicle or tractor stuck in mud. Roads constantly had water over them, but if it weren't for the roads, there would be absolutely no drainage at all.

Several attempts had been made to establish drainage districts to mitigate the problems. When brought to the public for an election, each time it failed. I had been one of the leaders in making those attempts. I had just been informed of the last drainage district failure when I found myself driving past Mr. Wood's house in my car. I turned around and parked in front of his house. I knocked on his door.

Mr. Wood was a friend of mine. We had suffered through much together, although we had never had any deeply meaningful conversations. In recent years we had talked more—mostly about the old days when he was young. He grew older by the day, but his eyes were still bright. They were blue and sparkling eyes permeated by a seemingly inextinguishable ray of hope. Men and women search lifetimes for the message in his eyes. I wanted to ask him how he obtained that precious treasure, but I knew he could never express it all in words.

He was eighty-two. His wife had died a few years back, and his leg had been amputated almost immediately after her death. His only son had died of a heart attack at the age of forty-two. His two grandsons had also died—one was killed in a car wreck and the other had died by suicide. No one of his blood would ever carry his name. It was terribly sad because the old man was proud and gentle and loving and wise. He fascinated me with his total awareness of the world and all the things happening in it. Withdrawal I could have understood, but he talked to me like a thirteen-year-old reaching adolescence. He was declarative about world politics, inquisitive about community affairs, concerned about the welfare of his neighbors. He was alive, and I didn't understand it.

Stories of the old days were his favorite pastime. We talked of World War I, the Great Depression, and World War II. We never talked about the great battles of either war or the causes of Wall Street's collapse. Instead, we talked about how these events affected the lives of people, his people, Americans in this local community. The old man began his empire during this period of time—an empire not in the sense of monetary riches but an empire of abundant life. It seemed he had never wasted a moment. I believe if he were given the chance to live his life over again, he would take it, simply because he enjoyed the whole affair tremendously the first time.

"I just can't tell you how good it is to see you, Kenneth," he said as he rolled and I walked into his living room. It was small with an old unused fireplace in it. His heat came from a gas space heater. He had pictures of his family as decorations over the old cheesecloth wallpaper, which was torn in a few places. The house smelled musty, but the smell was overtaken by blooming gardenias at every window. It reminded me of my boyhood when I would play with his grandson. I loved that smell.

"Have a seat, have a seat, Kenneth," Mr. Wood said excitedly as he gestured to a chair and smiled at me.

I sat down in an old easy chair that I thought was going to sink with me through the floor. It was obvious no one had been sitting there for a while.

"It sure is a beautiful spring day, isn't it?" he said. "I'd give a twenty-dollar bill to be able to walk out there and just look at the trees and smell the flowers." He kept the smile on his face and looked longingly out the window.

"Do you ever get to go outside, Mr. Wood?" I asked.

"Oh, sometimes Sam, my son-in-law, and my granddaughter, Amber, will help me get down the stairs and then roll me around the yard. I haven't been out this spring, though. But enough about me, my boy. What's on your mind?"

I thought about him not going outside. This spring had been exceptionally nice. Good weather for days on end—not too hot and not too cold. I had luxuriated in it, and he had not been able to experience its glory. This problem I had with the election looked petty in comparison.

"It's not much, Mr. Wood," I replied. "I'm just angry that this drainage district election didn't pass. I thought it would be good for the community, and I don't understand why people don't want to pay for a better place to live."

He looked at me for a moment and said, "Kenneth, did I ever tell you about the time I was county commissioner?"

"No, Mr. Wood, I didn't know you were in that position."

"Twenty years. I learned a lot about people and politics." With a smile and a gleam in his eyes, he looked directly into mine. "You can't predict them. About the time you think you got both of them figured out, they change on you."

"You can say that again."

"I will tell you that sometimes people are hardheaded and sometimes they have to be hit on the head by God through his righteous wrath before they get the message from the messenger. That, my boy, is as old as Jeremiah in the Bible."

He continued. "Now those of us who lead, we believe that logic and good sense will prevail when groups of people do things. It's true most of the time, but there are times when ignorance prevails, like when I was county commissioner. I had an old boy, Malcolm Davis, who wouldn't sell the county an easement for a road. We just needed a little corner of his property to make it wide enough for cars. There were even some questions on the title work about him even owning it. However, I dickered with him for about a month and finally condemned it. He told me he was going to take me to court. I just laughed at him and told him that ship had already sailed when I condemned it. Then he threatened me physically, told me he would find me one day when I wasn't looking and shoot me. I didn't pay attention to him. He knew I had a gun on me most of the time and besides that he was a coward."

"Did you get the easement?"

"Of course I did. It was at the intersection of this State Highway 231 and FM 1012. The condemnation court gave him less than we offered for it." He laughed. "That's the way it usually goes with such people." He looked at me, eyes twinkling.

"But here's the best part of that story, Kenneth. You know that convenience store and gas station at that intersection?"

"Yes, sir. I do. It's a busy place."

"That old boy got fifty times what he paid for that land when they bought it from him. It was all because his small piece of property made that intersection more conducive to high volumes of traffic and easy access to the rest of his property. He retired early. To this day, he still doesn't talk to me. I think it's because he was embarrassed about his behavior and can't bring himself to apologize to me. He knows he benefited by my vision."

"I see what you're trying to tell me."

"Yeah, son. You can't pay attention to ignorance and petty jealousies, or you're just like a dog chasing his tail. It never ends. Go on with that vision God has given you. Make it your destiny. You'll have a much more satisfying life. Let those people wallow in the mud of their despair until they see the light, and even then, some of them will not see it. Don't let them drag you down to their level."

"Do you think we will ever solve this drainage problem?" I asked.

"Certainly. But it may not be in your lifetime. What you are doing now is planting seeds. A seed of doubt with the ignorant ones who think they know everything but also know there is a problem. A seed of wisdom for those who have some knowledge and are seeking a solution but have not made up their mind. A seed of confidence for the people who are even more sure about the drainage district being the best option. Nothing that you do for the good of others is ever disregarded by our Almighty God. He nurtures it and blesses it and then brings it to life someday according to His timing."

I thought about this incremental approach to public policy, including the timing of the Creator and his creations. Was it better to move slowly along with the lack of knowledge and understanding, educating folks about certain issues and igniting their critical thinking? It would probably mean a lot of failures along the way just like the one I had experienced, but it also meant that something could break in the right direction as logic and enlightenment began to take root.

At some point, people would be ready to collectively do something about the drainage problem in some fashion, but only if they were informed about the problems and the solutions to them.

As he rambled, it was obvious that he was giving advice and encouragement for living. Confident about the vivacity of life, it almost seemed like he could never die. But death was there, and he knew it. Oh, how well he knew it! Not as outwardly apparent as his advice and encouragement were the implied exhortations of preparing for death. "Live full," he was saying, "live life well, with fervor, with graciousness, with love, and you will be prepared for death."

I knew the old man was not scared to die. He had lived an abundant life. He knew the secret. It was there in his eyes. They still had vision in them, and they knew their destination. That is when I got inklings of my own vision.

I thought about things that meant a lot to me and realized I had arrived at them incrementally. It was a revelation. I would set a goal with some objectives and then move toward them bit by bit over time. The drainage district was not an incremental thing. It was too big for people in the community to understand the scope and all the moving parts. However, talking about drainage and its importance, educating folks little by little, was the way to solve the drainage problem. There were many other quality-of-life problems I wanted to solve and the best platform for me to do it was to become a county commissioner.

I knew my wife, Angie, would be excited about it. She was a social animal and the kind of person who would enjoy the good and bad interactions of local politics. After I said goodbye to Mr. Wood, I went home to tell her. She was sitting in the living room watching the evening news.

"Honey," I said, "I need to talk to you about something."

"Just a minute, I want to see what this congressman is saying about the environmental bill the House just passed," she answered.

I knew it would be a good moment for me to tell her I wanted to get into politics. She was passionate about certain issues. She thought a lot of them could be solved through good politics and government. I agreed with her, but didn't have her missionary zeal.

She turned off the TV and smiled as she turned and looked me in the eyes.

"Okay, sweetie, what do you want to tell me?"

"I'm going to run for county commissioner."

The smile went away, and she had a curious, thoughtful look in her eyes. She seemed to be a million miles away.

I finally said, "Did you hear me, Angie?"

She came out of her trance and said, "Yes, I heard you, and I was trying to figure out some campaign slogans and how you could get elected. I'm excited."

I knew it. She may as well have been the one running, but she didn't like to speak in front of people. She was always busy behind the scenes. She had really pushed me to be on the school board. I served for six years and was the president for three of those years, and all the time she was whispering something in my ear about how I should do that volunteer job. I didn't mind it but there were times I had to ask her to let up.

"You know the current commissioner, Norman White, is retiring, and there will be a lot of people lining up to run for the job," I said.

"Yes, but you were on the school board and in a leadership position. This is the largest school district in this precinct. You were elected by a sizable majority. A lot of people liked the job you did and wanted you to stay on the board."

I had not given it that much analysis. This was one of the reasons I was running... Angie Howell. There would be no better campaign manager or advisor I could have in this office.

"You know I'll have to resign from my job to take this job full-time," I said to her. "The salary is close to what I'm making now, but I'll have to pay for all the campaign expenses."

"Oh well now, we can get donors—and let me tell you, I have a list already in my mind."

I shook my head. It was further confirmation I had made the right decision.

I really just wanted to get the drainage in this county fixed, and now I was in serious campaign mode. I had to remind myself to keep my feet on the ground.

The campaign did go well. We started off with a bang. Angie and I had two teenage children. They helped quite a bit. My two brothers and their families got on the bandwagon, and I started actually having a good time talking to old friends and many people I never had met.

There were always strange folks, though. Like the time a man I knew casually came to me at a campaign event and told me he didn't like federal government grants.

I said, "Mr. Ford, why don't you like them?" "

Too many strings attached," he replied.

"Okay, it is our money we send to Washington, and they are sending it back to us to be used for a specific purpose that 99% of the time helps our community.

"I just don't like them telling us what to do. For instance, when the highway funding came up years ago, they wouldn't give our state, Texas, any money unless we passed mandatory seat belt laws."

I gave him a puzzled look and said, "What's wrong with mandatory seat belt laws?"

"Well, nothing, dadblameit. I think people should wear seat belts, but the federal government shouldn't be telling us to do it."

"Okay, who's going to tell them?"

"Ourselves."

I was stumped. I guess he thought that everyone would voluntarily wear their seatbelt.

"Well, Mr. Ford, I don't know what to tell you. It would be nice if everyone would do the right thing, but that's why we have laws, incentives and disincentives to keep from harming ourselves and other people."

"You're right. That's the way it should be."

Then he walked away, and I was checking my smartphone to see if Scotty was ready to beam me back up to the Starship Enterprise.

Then Linda Richardson, the lady who wanted to know what I was going to do about the stray animals, changing the hours at the dump, and United Nations Resolution 546.

I said, "Ms. Richardson, let me say, I sympathize with you about these stray animals, and we do need to make partnerships with the municipalities in the county to assist us with animal control. I've already been talking to several of the city managers. As far as the dump hours are concerned, I don't think we can change them. My predecessor has worked hard to make them convenient for everyone. And concerning United Nations Resolution 546, I'm afraid I don't know anything about it."

She responded, "Well, I have thirty cats, ten dogs, and fourteen horses, and I can't just keep adding to them. They come wandering up to my place in the woods. I don't know what to do with them. I need some help paying for their feed. And don't call me Ms.—I'm not a liberal. Call me Mrs. My husband died five years ago. Now, who was your predecessor?"

"Norman White."

"Yeah, I know he's the guy you will be replacing, but I need to know your predecessor."

I know I had a blank look on my face. This was a puzzle I could not solve. Then Mr. Ford stood behind Mrs. Richardson and tapped her on the shoulder. She turned around and saw him, gave him a smile with a few missing teeth, and hugged him, saying, "I thought I smelled you in here, you old crook."

I eased out of the way while they had their reunion. I walked over and stood beside Angie, who was talking to County Judge Melvin Kirk. He had been in office for eight years. He was mostly a politician. Melvin liked to see which way the political winds were blowing. That was the way he made decisions. He had very little courage to take any action which may anger his voter base. There were also some questions about his intelligence. I think he had enough smarts to weather the storm, but he depended on other people for ideas to solve major problems and to cast a vision. He was also a prolific flirt.

"…you're such a beautiful woman, and I know you will be an asset to Kenneth in his role as commissioner," I heard Melvin saying as I joined the group.

She looked demurely at Judge Kirk and said, "Well, thank you Melvin. You're so sweet. If you'll excuse me, I need to talk to Kenneth."

She semi-escorted me to a corner of the room and said, "Thanks for the rescue. How does that man function? I tried to talk to him about a variety of policy issues that could help the people of this county and all he could do is talk me up like he was going to ask me for a date?'

I couldn't resist and asked, "Did he?"

She got an exasperated look, then glared at me, and I knew I was in trouble. She then said, "No, but if you ask me another smartass question like that, I'll still go on that date with you this Saturday—but it won't have a happy ending."

"I'm sorry," I said. "I had to come over here and talk to you to make sure all of this is real. I just talked to two people who I think may be in another space-time continuum."

She laughed heartily at this remark. I knew I was back in her good graces.

After laughing a lot, she turned thoughtful, "I did not realize how many different kinds of people there are in our county until we started campaigning. All that big picture thinking we have discussed ad infinitum over the years just doesn't resonate too much with a lot of voters."

I smiled and said, "Right. Even the meanings of certain words do not mean the same thing to them as they do to us, like 'predecessor'."

"What?"

"It's a long story, but I do know we are going to have to set our sights a little lower as far as goals and objectives are concerned while I'm in office. It's important that I get elected or there will be no platform for the bigpicture ideas.

"Right now, let's focus on me getting elected. I have four opponents. For anyone, including me, to get a majority of the votes in this precinct is problematic come March. There will probably be a runoff. Right now, Curtis Fontenot and I will probably be the top two receiving votes. Endorsements from the other candidates will mean a lot. I will buddy up to them, but you will be the icing on the cake with your charm."

"So now I have charm. Is that hooker-like charm or professional-accomplished-woman charm?'

"Okay, touché. Just remember the happy ending at the end of the date can work both ways." She just smiled at me.

"We need to tell everyone helping us to always ask people to vote for me. It's very simple but many candidates just do not do it. It's fundamental in America. People who vote consider it a precious right. But they are not going to vote for you unless you ask them. They don't want you to take them for granted. I know we will not see every voter, but we will see enough that their votes and their circle-of-influence votes will make the difference.

The campaign got hotter and hotter. One candidate dropped out and endorsed me. I thanked Angie because I knew she had talked to him after I did. He definitely liked her more than me. One night I got a telephone call from Ronnie Adams, a prominent businessman from Lyric. He lived in our precinct and his business was in our precinct. He started talking to me about the county road that ran in front of some of his vacant property. He was going on about the terrible condition of the road and wanted to know what I would do about it once I was elected. I knew where this was going, and I was pretty sure of the outcome.

I responded to him, "Ronnie, it is my intention to pave every road in our precinct that needs to be paved. Of course, I have a budget. I intend to analyze each road by objective criteria based on several factors, such as traffic use and the degree of deterioration. Then I will rank them based on that criteria and then pave them by their order in the ranking. Then I will use my entire paving budget on those ranked roads."

"Sounds complicated to me," said Ronnie, "why don't you pave the roads for the property owners who are paying the most taxes?"

"Because once those owners pay those taxes, it is for their elected representatives to decide what is fair for all the people they are elected to serve. It no longer belongs to those property owners. That is why we live in a democracy. It's about being fair and equal."

"Boy, you have a lot to learn. See you later." He hung up the phone.

I knew I wouldn't get his vote and the votes from his considerable sphere of influence.

I sat looking straight ahead out the window when I finished that conversation. It had been raining for about two hours. Water was backing up in the road ditches and soon would be over all the county roads where I lived. I realized that I had not discussed drainage during the campaign with the exception of one time. I was at a Rotary Club meeting. I brought my PowerPoint presentation. It had maps and succinctly showed how the county could use flood water detention, ditches, and existing creeks and rivers to manage the drainage in the county, if we could only be unified in our approach and look at the overall picture of drainage in each watershed of the county. There were about thirty people in the meeting. While I was making the presentation, four were talking to other people, sixteen were looking at their smartphones, three were nodding off after the carbohydrate-rich meal, and about seven were paying attention to me.

Sheriff Hunter Eagle got up to talk after me. He discussed in great detail his recent apprehension of a man who was wanted for a marijuana possession charge and the fifty-mile car chase by Sheriff Eagle's department and two other nearby county sheriffs' departments. Sheriff Eagle had the rapt attention of all thirty people. I was actually wondering how much public money had been spent apprehending this man who had no other criminal charges, was non-violent, and would probably spend very little time in jail for the marijuana charge but would spend a lot of time in jail for resisting arrest. It was convoluted, but it was an attention-getter.

The rain continued through the night. At 3:00 a.m. I woke up and heard it pouring down. The lightning and thunder were tremendous. Occasionally, I could see through the dark with a lightning flash and saw my front yard full of water. I couldn't go back to sleep. This could be my attention-getter. The election was only two weeks away. If I won this primary election and the probable runoff, I would be in office. Our county was a one-party county with a few exceptions.

There was no candidate running in the other party's primary for this commissioner position. I began making a list of the locations in the county where I knew roads would be flooded. I was going to take pictures. My friend Slim Page had a jacked-up four-wheel drive pickup and told me he would help me with my campaign if I ever needed him. At 6:30 a.m., when the sunrise gave enough light to assess the damage, I knew I had something. Water was everywhere. I called Slim, told him about my idea, and he told me he would be at my house in about an hour.

When Slim drove up on the county road, it looked like the wake of a boat. I was out on the porch and took a video of it. I had donned my duck hunting waders and went to meet him. He was smiling from ear to ear.

"Kenneth, I got to by God tell you, this is exciting," Slim said as I got in the truck. "This is goin' make these people understan' that we got to do somethin' about all this damn water."

"Right, Slim. Let's get to it," I responded.

We went to every place on the list. This was the first time I had spent this much time with Slim. I had twenty places in the County where I wanted to go and get some shots of the flooding. They did not disappoint. We saw road washouts, culverts almost taken out of the road, houses flooded, and vehicles abandoned in the ditches. It had been a terrific storm.

We also served as a two-man rescue unit. When Slim saw someone in trouble, he automatically stopped to see if he could be of assistance. He had chains, straps, and cables. He also had a winch on the front of his truck. We pulled cars and trucks out of ditches and winched two of them away from a culvert where they had hit high center. The drivers could not see the edge of the culvert for the water and missed the driveway. Each vehicle was drivable after being pulled out.

I was struck by the generosity of Slim. I had known him for a long time. I knew he was kind, but he loved helping all these folks using his truck during this disaster. Even the wreckers were unable to perform the service he provided because they were not as high off the ground. He had two coolers of water and Gatorade. He would give it to people without them asking for it. I also heard about his entire personal life. He called his wife, "Mama". Her real name was Geri. They had five kids. The oldest was a boy of twelve and youngest was a three-year-old girl. I asked him what all of his family was doing today.

"Now, Mama is at home with the three girls. They are makin' sandwiches and cookies for the first responders. The two boys are at the fire station helpin' with equipment and handin' out bottled water and food to people," Slim said with a big toothy smile.

"Slim, I thought Geri was recovering from surgery," I responded.

"Yeh, she had some female problems and is goin' be all right. We not goin' have any more babies, but lawd, that's all right with me. That don't mean we can't have a roll in the hay three or four times a week, but we gotta wait a while to start that recreation." He looked at me with that toothy grin and then laughed heartily when he saw the dumbfounded look on my face.

I got two hundred quality pictures. Slim had taken some of me hooking up vehicles to the chain, hip deep in water. I came home and started picking out the best of all the pictures for my PowerPoint presentation. I included several of Slim and several of me helping people during the flood.

I was right. The pictures of the flood were attention-getters. I made a book of them and showed them to people when I couldn't use the PowerPoint presentation. I also showed the pictures on my phone to those who were interested. I had five campaign events before the election and showed them the problems we had because of insufficient and poorly planned and designed drainage. I had people telling me their sad stories of flooded houses and vehicles and how inconvenient and costly the whole event had been. I made notes on my phone of these individual stories because I knew all of these voters would gradually change their minds when we didn't have any more flood events and things seemed normal. I even had quotes from each one of the commissioners and the county judge supportive of doing something about drainage. I knew they would quickly change their minds when it came to spending money.

My last campaign event was during the last week of early voting. I could sense momentum in picking up votes. At this last event, Ronnie Adams showed up with Curtis Fontenot. When it came time for Curtis to speak, Ronnie lobbed him some softball questions about development and how it helped the county provide jobs and tax base for the community so that taxpayers would not have to pay higher taxes. It was the same old shell game everyone used, even me. Then Ronnie lobbed him another question about how roads were more important in some places than others and a hell of a lot more important than spending money on drainage that only benefitted developers. I had him. I knew Ronnie would try to paint me with this brush through Curtis. However, I had to word my answers so that I would not fall into this trap.

Ronnie had Fred Reynolds ask me questions. He stood up and said, "Mr. Howell, I want to know why you keep telling people in our precinct why drainage is more important than roads," Fred asked.

I paused for effect, looked Fred in the eye and said, "Fred, I have never said drainage is more important than roads. You and Ronnie are making that scenario up in your own minds. I emphasized drainage recently because poor drainage has cost many people in this precinct a lot of grief and money—even as recently as just two weeks ago. The county can do something to stop this incessant flooding we have on a regular basis. Maybe you, Ronnie, and Curtis haven't been as close to it as I was when I was helping people get their vehicles out of the ditch with Slim Page."

There was a round of applause. Fred turned red, as did Ronnie and Curtis. He sat down. There were no other questions for me. I gave a short speech thanking people for coming to the event and asked them to vote for me. I didn't have to give the PowerPoint presentation. The confrontation with Fred was enough.

On primary election day, I visited each polling place. I was confident I would make the runoff. I had momentum, and I had Angie. She had found a way to get everybody to the polls who wanted to vote for me. She had people strategically placed throughout the precinct to hand out election paraphernalia and give rides. Early voting was setting records and I wondered if that was a good sign. I had been getting a lot of good feedback about the drainage issue. I knew I had been blessed. In general, we did not get major rain events in February. This one and the way I had portrayed it as a salient issue gave me a lot of momentum at the right time. I was thankful that it gave me a platform to make a case for this needed improvement in our community. The other side of that coin was the misery it had given to a lot of people. But I knew we could eliminate that misery if we just did some planning and did something that would be effective for generations to come.

I won the election without a runoff. I got 50.9% of the vote. Curtis Fontenot was next with 41.1 %. The other two candidates split the remaining votes almost evenly. I was stunned. I never thought I would win without a runoff. It validated the campaign and my vision for good community development. I was elated. Angie was more than elated. She had a big victory party, and a lot of people came and celebrated with us into the wee hours. In my subconscious, I knew hard work was ahead, and there would be a lot of hills and valleys. I was ready for the challenge. I just hoped I could manage it.

Managing was the key word. My predecessor, Norman White, was a nice man who performed well with county politics, but managing his everyday duties was not his strong suit. His management style with constituents was to take care of the loudest person who would vote and who had the largest circle of influence. I was not naïve. I could not change that approach immediately, but it had to change. There were roads, drainage, and environmental and safety issues in my precinct that Norman had been neglecting for years. His management style with employees was a perfect example of the Peter Principle, which basically states that some organizations do not work effectively because people are promoted to their level of incompetence. The current road foreman at my precinct had been an excellent Gradall operator. However, as road foreman, he did not know how to train employees, schedule work assignments, or accomplish much in one day. It was a mess and had been for years. I started untangling it when I appeared the first day.

In addition to my precinct, I had to consider the strategic planning and budget for the county with the other commissioners and the county judge. When I walked into my first meeting of the commissioners' court, I could feel the air heavy with local politics. Everyone in the room was positioning themselves for something they needed from the taxpayers of the county. There was an item on the agenda where the county judge wanted an explanation from the state district judge about why he wanted to add an extra unbudgeted employee to his staff. The exchange started well enough but grew tense as the two men began arguing with each other. Finally they started shouting, and the county judge called on the sheriff's deputy who was assigned to the court to escort the state district judge out of the room. You could hear a pin drop after that altercation. Other items discussed after the dustup were rather mundane, comparatively speaking. At last, we came to the final item on the agenda, for an appointment to a community development grant committee at the regional council of governments. It piqued my interest. I asked the county judge the purpose of the committee, and he explained that they rank grant applications for federal government funding. The judge then asked me if I was interested in being the appointee. I looked around at the other commissioners and each one of them was looking down at paperwork, obviously not interested in it. I said, "Well, sure, if nobody else wants to do it."

Commissioner Blake said, "I move we appoint our outstanding new Commissioner Howell."

Commissioner Payne said, "I second the motion."

It was a unanimous vote and just like that, I was on a committee I knew nothing about.

Eight months later, I was in Houston at the offices of the Houston-Galveston Area Council of Governments in the conference room with several other local elected officials from surrounding county and municipal governments. It was the meeting of the Community Development Block Grant Regional Review Committee, or RRC. I had finally got some sense of the purpose of the committee to which I was appointed in such an inauspicious way by my other commissioners. As with many other things in our county government, I don't believe my comrades understood the importance of this committee or really cared about it. The RRC would be distributing several million dollars of federal funds to local governments to enhance infrastructure such as repairing or building water lines, sewer lines, roads, and drainage structures in low- to moderate-income areas. I felt like I had found a gold mine. Not only could our county apply for these funds, but municipalities in my precinct could apply for them. They were ranked by the RRC on a point system. I had a drainage project I wanted to do in my precinct that coincided with a similar need in two municipalities located in my precinct. I talked to each of their city managers, and they got approval from their respective city councils. We possibly could get a million dollars for drainage work in my precinct.

I tried not to show my excitement to the other members of the RRC because I knew it would look self-serving, and if I had learned anything in politics, it was a cardinal rule to make any initiative look good for "all the people." My fellow RRC members had elected me vice-chairman. I used this position to make qualified and reasonable statements about the priorities for funding. There was good debate about these priorities. In the end, I was able to convince the RRC to place drainage in the highest ranking along with water and sewer improvements.

The grading and ranking point system was designed to be as objective as possible in selecting the final grantees. I could not rank my county's project and the two municipalities in my precinct. However, I could rank all the others. All projects had base scores based on their level of poverty and whether they had received previous funding. I soon discovered that by scoring the subjective criteria on all the projects very low, except the projects of interest to me, the chances of the latter receiving funds were much higher. This also especially helped if there were other people on the RRC who used the same method. I had deduced this much on my own. However, at a previous meeting six months earlier when we set up the scoring system, another commissioner, Janice Shirley from Galveston County, mentioned it to me.

"I think there is a math problem with this system," she casually said to me while we were breaking for lunch.

"Yes, I noticed it. I'm not sure what to do about it," I answered.

"There's nothing you can do except use it to the advantage of the constituents who elected you to office," she said, winking and smiling.

I nodded my head. I knew exactly what she meant. You scratch my back, and I'll scratch your back, and we'll help the people who elected us. We continued to talk about what we were doing as commissioners in our respective counties. However, what was left unsaid was more important to me. She was an ally.

We had to hear presentations from each project. This was done by either an elected official or a staff member of the political jurisdiction. Projects which were providing a first-time service, such as centralized wastewater collection—what most people know of as sanitary sewer--were given a higher priority than others.

One presentation was given by a deep, gravel-voiced public works director, Ralph Jones, from the City of San Leon. It was a first-time sanitary sewer service for a low-income area of town. I knew this project was in Commissioner Shirley's precinct.

Mr. Jones said, "I know most of you folks sitting here today probably have a good sewer system. You're either on a city sewer system or private septic system that probably works pretty good. I want you to look at these here pictures."

Pictures that appeared on a screen in front of us showed black and green mucky, watery material in different places throughout the municipality. It was not easy on the mind or stomach.

"Now you see right here, we got a school playground not very far from this crap," Jones told us, using a laser pointer to show us on the picture. "This is the result of old septic systems not working properly, and also having too many of them in this blackland clay, which is everywhere in Galveston County. That's why we need to get sewer lines to these folks to get rid of this crappy situation."

He showed us the next picture and pointed out a water line being repaired and some of the black and green mud around it.

"Now this is just horrible. The water district is repairing a line, doing the best they can to keep this crap out of the hole but some of it gets there. With these water leaks, backflow pressure makes this fecal material go into the water line. Of course, we tell people to boil water, but this infiltration into the water system could have been happening before the leak was found by the water district. It's not sanitary and not fit to drink. In other words, these people are drinking their own shit."

Unlike the rest of the committee members with their heads down, the committee chair and I had been watching Mr. Jones make his presentation. My eyes went wide open, and my eyebrows were raised. The committee chair had the same expression, and his mouth was agape. I looked at Commissioner Shirley and even though she had her head down, there was a slight grin on her face.

Jones continued, "That concludes my presentation, ladies and gentlemen, I'll be glad to answer any questions."

A member of the committee, an annoying commissioner from Matagorda County, asked the same question to Mr. Jones that he had asked to every other applicant, "What is your tax rate?"

Unlike many of the other applicants, Mr. Jones said, "The City of San Leon tax rate doesn't have a damn thing to do with this project. Regulations require that we must apply for these funds because the water district can't apply for them. We're trying to get them some money. If you'll look at our application, you'll see that they only have a $50,000 emergency reserve, and they have the highest water and sewer rates of any applicant here today. People, we need this money!"

I was beginning to like this guy. He wasn't belligerent. He was straight to the point. The asinine question of a tax rate had nothing to do with the need for this project. There were no other questions for Ralph Jones. Commissioner Shirley still had the grin on her face. I ranked this project high.

The presentation for all of the projects in my precinct went very well. I saw Commissioner Shirley look at me when it was time to score each project of interest to me. She gave me a slight nod of the head when she finished scoring. There was a possibility that fourteen projects would receive funding. This depended on approval of funding by the U. S. Congress.

After the meeting, I told Commissioner Shirley I enjoyed meeting her and working with her. She reciprocated with the same remarks. We shook hands and nothing else was said. Two days later, I saw the result of the scoring. The City of San Leon and the Galveston County projects ranked in the top two places and the three projects in my precinct were third, fourth and fifth. I felt like I had bet the house in seven card stud on three of a kind with an ace high flush staring me right in the face, and I won the hand. I yelled in my office, "Yes!!!" My assistant heard me and walked in to see me looking at the computer. She said, "Are you all right?"

"Yes!!!" I yelled, "We just got about a million dollars in grant money to do those drainage projects."

"Kenneth," she responded, "you never cease to amaze with your excitement over such a mundane thing as drainage."

"I know, I know, but it is just fundamental around here and improving it will make our lives better."

"Whatever you say," she said, then smiled and walked away.

The wheels of bureaucracy turn slowly, I learned, but within a year, we were requesting bids to do the construction on these three projects, which had been designed to complement each other. Two of the bids came in under budget and the one for my precinct was over by $10,000. I had the money to cover it in my precinct budget. Construction started in May and was expected to be completed by mid-August on all three projects. We had very few problems with acquiring the easements necessary for the projects because I had already been discussing it with the landowners before we started the application process. The municipalities had followed suit. All of the projects were completed on time except for one municipality. Because it was at the top of the drainage contour, we were not too concerned about it. The project was completed in mid-September.

As if to prove we had done the right thing, rain began to fall after the last inspection, and it continued for thirty-six hours straight. The communities that had suffered the most from flooding in my precinct did not see one drop of water in a house from flooding nor did any of the roads. The combination of detention ponds, ditches, and redirecting water flow had worked as designed by our engineers.

My phone was ringing all day long the day the floodwater receded. People were thanking me for constructing a drainage system that worked and for getting funds to pay for it. I was high as a kite. I went to see my friend Mr. Wood.

"Well, Kenneth Howell," he exclaimed, "you are a sight for sore eyes. I've been needing a little company, and you are just the person I need to talk to!" He was grinning from ear to ear just like last time. I had to laugh. He was such a joyful person.

"Mr. Wood, I must tell you, you inspire me. When I was here about three years ago, I decided to run for commissioner after my talk with you."

"I know. I voted for you," he responded.

"Well, I'm sorry I haven't been by to see you, but it's a busy job as you know."

"Yes, I know, but it looks to me like it paid off for all of us. I noticed when we had that tropical storm, the drainage worked perfectly around here. I sat on my porch and watched it. I said to myself, 'Kenneth is probably out there dancing naked in the rain.'" He laughed with that high-pitched "heh, heh, heh...."

I looked at him. He was eighty-five—still soaking up every morsel of life he could get. The wheelchair had moved slower this time, and his shoulders were more bent. Some of the light had gone out of his eyes, but he was rejoicing with me. I liked my job as commissioner. I was able to make some lasting changes in my community, just like he did. It was just as much his victory as it was mine. In his own way, he had given me vision, and that vision had provided me with a destiny. I knew I could do this job.

We talked awhile longer. I told him how I had received the political support and, more importantly, the financial support I needed to do the major drainage project. I also told him how my organizational skills had helped make the precinct employees more efficient and effective. He continued to smile and nod his head.

As I was leaving, he grabbed my hand and said, "Kenneth, I'm not much longer for this world. I know it's my time. I'm ready to go. Thank you for coming by to see me. I want to ask if you would say a few words at my funeral."

"Of course, Mr. Wood. It would be an honor for me."

He squeezed my hand and said, "I'll tell Dora. She'll see that it's done."

As I drove home, I thought about his influence on my life. It was hard to put into words. I dismissed it as a present thought, but like an earworm it kept coming back that evening while I was talking with Angie about our visit and about getting ready for the next election. It was only a year away, and I had to get started on it.

At ten the next morning, Dora, Mr. Wood's daughter, called me. She said, "Kenneth, Daddy died this morning about seven o'clock. His big heart finally gave out."

I was not surprised. He had known he was about to die when he talked to me. I was speechless for a moment.

Dora continued, "He called me yesterday and told me he wanted you to speak at his funeral. Will you do it?"

I could only answer her with the words I said to him, "It would be my honor."

Two days later I stood in front of a crowd of three hundred people. I had no idea Lew Wood had that many friends and acquaintances. He didn't, as I was to find out. I did see Malcolm Davis, his old nemesis, in attendance. Before the service began, I talked to many of them who I knew from my first campaign. Few of them personally knew him. Their common statement was, "I'm here because I have a lot of respect for Mr. Wood and his family. We're going to miss his vision." Then the words came to me. I knew what I needed to say.

I told some good stories about him from my personal experience, and some that other people had told me. I then talked about my relationship with him and how, from the time I was a boy, he had inspired me to become more than I was on each occasion he spoke to me. I told them how I was always looking ahead after I talked to him, even though I wasn't sure what I was going to do. I knew there was something out there that needed to be done, and I was the one destined to do it. I closed with a scripture from the Bible, 1 Corinthians 13:12-13 The Apostle Paul wrote it to the Christian church at Corinth when he was trying to get them to understand the deep meaning of living with each other.

I said, "I know this may not be the exact interpretation of this scripture from a theologian's point of view, but it does describe the life of Lew Wood to me. He was always looking ahead. He had a lot of faith, hope, and love and moved through life with a vision because he knew he was going somewhere. He gave that priceless attitude to me. Here's the scripture: 'Now we see things imperfectly, like puzzling reflections in a mirror, but then we will see everything with perfect clarity. All that I know now is partial and incomplete, but then I will know everything completely, just as God now knows me completely. Three things will last forever—faith, hope, and love—and the greatest of these is love'. Lew Wood now knows everything completely, just as God knows him completely."

I won the next election because I got the most votes, but I don't think it was just the votes. I think it was the vision. Mr. Wood knew how to inspire me. He practiced the three things that last forever—faith, hope and love. He led me with his wisdom to have vision that was practical and necessary for our community—his people and my people, who believed in what we could do, hoped the best for all of us, and most of all, loved each other.

THE STOREKEEPER

It was a hot, East Texas, summer day in June of 1962, and John Harvey was in heaven. Heaven, of course, was being eight years old, fresh out of school, and playing with his best friend, Ike Andrus. He and Ike had ridden their bicycles up and down the blacktop country roads by Ike's house, played a bicycle-modified version of polo, and stolen a few plums from the tree in Ike's aunt's backyard. It was marvelous. He couldn't remember ever feeling happier.

Ike was always good at finding new fun things to do even if they were a little dangerous and sometimes forbidden. Today was no exception. Ike had begun digging a cave under the old chicken house behind his grandfather's small but nice house. John knew Ike loved to dig caves and was good at it, but this one was a real masterpiece. He had lifted the boards off the floor of the chicken house and had started the cave there. It was already three feet deep and had enough room for both of them. John and Ike got in and Ike pulled the boards over them.

"See, John," Ike whispered as he lit a candle, "we can have our own clubhouse here and nobody can bother us."

That sounded good to John, but he really didn't know who would be bothering them. Unless it was Ike's grandfather, Mr. Andrus. He and Ike's father ran the local general store. Mr. Andrus had always struck John as a kindly old gentleman. But that bothered Ike--the kindly part, that is. It meant he always wanted Ike to do what was right and, naturally, that was not always what Ike really wanted to do. Take the cave, for example. John knew Mr. Andrus probably had not given Ike permission to dig underneath his chicken house. Sometimes it made John a little uneasy when Ike came up with some of his daredevil and unusual schemes. As the stay in the cave became boring, John was getting the impression this was another one of those schemes.

"Ike, where are you?" It was Mr. Andrus.

"Uh-oh," Ike said, "we'll have to stay here, John, until Granddad leaves." John knew it. This was another one of Ike's daring schemes. He hated to get in trouble, and this looked like trouble all right. He didn't move, though. He didn't want Mr. Andrus to catch them.

"Ike!" His voice was growing more distant now.

"I think he's in the front yard--let's go," Ike whispered as he flipped up the floorboards to the chicken house. He and John cautiously walked to the door. Peeking through a crack, they could see no one near. Ike opened the door and ran toward the back of his Granddad's house. John was right behind him. When they reached the garage, they saw Mr. Andrus around the corner. John's heart went to his throat. He knew they had had it now.

"Ike, what have you been doing?" Mr. Andrus said, "I've been hollering at you for ten minutes."

"We've been playing, Granddad," Ike answered innocently.

"Well, get in there and wash up," he told them. "Your grandma has lunch on the table for you boys."

That sounded good to John. Mr. Andrus was none the wiser about the cave, and John always enjoyed Grandma Andrus's cooking. Things were looking good.

As they ate lunch, Ike gobbled his food like it was his last meal. Mr. and Mrs. Andrus ate slowly. John watched all three of them as he ate, and they talked. Ike didn't act anything like his grandparents. John knew there was a lot of difference in their ages, but it seemed like Ike somehow just didn't have something they had--he somehow didn't seem to care about anybody or anything but himself.

Ike finished his lunch and said, "I'm going to the store, Grandma, Granddad."

"Aren't you going to wait for John?" Mr. Andrus asked.

"You ready, John?" Ike queried.

"No, can't you see he's eating?" Grandma Andrus replied.

"Well, come on over when you get finished," and with that Ike bounded out of the room.

"That boy!" Grandma Andrus sounded exasperated.

"Go ahead and finish, John," Mr. Andrus sighed.

"Ike probably won't do anything but get into trouble over there anyhow."

John was surprised to hear Mr. Andrus say that. After all, Ike was his grandson.

"John, do you ever get into any trouble at school?" Mr. Andrus asked.

"I try not to, Mr. Andrus," he answered. "I don't like to get in trouble."

"I wish I could say that about Ike," he sighed. "It seems like he's in trouble at least once a week up there."

Mr. Andrus stared at the wall for quite a while as John continued eating.

"You know, John, Ike needs to learn like you to stay out of trouble," Mr. Andrus finally said.

John couldn't help but ask, "What do you mean, Mr. Andrus?"

"I mean he needs to learn responsibility. Learning to be responsible for your actions--the way you treat other people, the way you discipline yourself, the way you take care of possessions--that's what growing up and living is all about."

John thought to himself. He had heard that word "responsibility" before. He thought it had to do with things like his mother telling him he was the only one who could make sure his room stayed clean—that was the word she had used when she told him that.

"Yes, John, if I hadn't been taught how to be responsible when I was young, I wouldn't have been able to own and run my store," he explained. "It takes a lot of responsibility."

John understood. He had often heard his parents and other people say that Mr. Andrus was a good man.

"It just doesn't seem that Ike understands responsibility. We've asked him not to do things like ride his bicycle down the wrong way on the highway and not to dig caves without our permission. But he does it anyway. We don't want him to get hurt, but we especially don't want him to grow up and be irresponsible to other people like he did just a few minutes ago when he left you, his friend and guest, just sitting here."

Mr. Andrus was getting a little boring, but he was right about that last part. John didn't appreciate Ike getting up and leaving him. It made him feel awkward.

John had finished eating. He thanked Grandma Andrus for the meal and told her he always liked her cooking. He told Mr. Andrus that he was going to find Ike. He walked out of the house and was headed toward the store when he started hearing raised voices and then suddenly some screaming. He ran behind the store and saw Ike receiving the business end of his father's thin belt.

Ike's mother walked up next to him and put her hand on his shoulder. She told John that he had better go home because Ike wouldn't be allowed to play the rest of the day.

John seated himself on his bicycle and started toward his house. The day was not so bright now. The sun was still shining, but John didn't feel so good. He thought that it might have something to do with what Mr. Andrus had told him and with Ike getting a whipping. Trouble was something John always wanted to avoid, and he wondered why Ike was seldom able to do it. He and Ike were different; there was no doubt about that.

"It must be responsibility," he said aloud to himself.

It was a mile to John's house. He had made the trip down State Highway 278 many times. He rode on the left side of the road looking at the traffic, as his mother had instructed him. She wanted to make sure the cars could see him and that he could see the cars. She told him to do the same when he walked, too. He could ride on the highway if no cars were coming, but then had to move to the grassy shoulder whenever a car appeared. The pavement was only twenty feet wide for the northbound and southbound lanes. Fortunately, there usually wasn't much traffic.

The Texas sun was hot but not as hot as it would be getting later in the summer. Still, the hot asphalt was beginning to make his journey more difficult as it stuck to the tires and started slowing down his pedaling. Then he felt it get easier, but the bicycle was slowing down. He looked down at the chain, and it had broken. He pulled off to the shoulder. It scared him a little. He had never walked all the way home from Ike's, and he hadn't yet gotten very far. Now he would have to push his bicycle and walk the rest of the way. That meant he would have to do it on the grassy shoulder, which would be tough going.

He grabbed the handlebars, determined to make it home. A car going his southbound direction slowed down as it saw him and then speeded back up. His mother had told him not to accept rides with any strangers. He was getting a little more scared. About five minutes later, another southbound car slowed and then stopped up ahead of him on the shoulder. As he kept walking, the driver rolled his window down and said, "Do you need a ride?" John didn't look at him, just shook his head and kept walking. The driver slowly started driving along the road and said to John, "What's the matter, got a busted chain?" John just kept walking. He nodded and noticed that the driver had pulled up a little more and stopped his car. He craned his head out the window to look for oncoming traffic, then opened the door, got out of the car, and walked toward John.

John didn't stop. He was getting anxious, like he had when he got lost in the woods one day. His heart was beating fast. The man was smiling at him and seemed to want to help him, but John was uneasy. The man said, "My name is Bob. What's your name?" He looked about as old as John's father, and John thought it was weird that he didn't call himself "Mister" Something instead of Bob.

John just kept on walking. Bob said, "I can give you a ride and we can put your bike in the back seat." He then put his hands on the handlebars.

John was becoming frantic. He didn't like what the man was doing. Suddenly, he heard another vehicle pull up behind him and he turned around. It was Ike's Granddad. John kept his hands on the handlebars and Bob took his off. Bob looked at Mr. Andrus as he got out of his pickup and Bob said immediately, "I was just trying to help the boy. It looks like he has a busted chain."

Mr. Andrus looked at the man. In all the time John had known Mr. Andrus, he had never seen that look on his face. Not only was it stern, but he looked angry. John thought he might hit Bob. Mr. Andrus replied, "I know the boy, his parents, and where he lives. I'll take care of him. You can be on your way." Mr. Andrus continued to stare at Bob until Bob ran across the highway, got in his car, and sped away.

Mr. Andrus put his hand on John's shoulder and asked, "Are you all right, John?"

"Yessir," John replied as he looked up at Mr. Andrus. "I didn't like that man."

"You've got a right to not like him. He's not a nice man. You did the right thing by not encouraging him. If this ever happens again with a strange man, you run and get away from him just as quick as you can. Just leave your bicycle."

John nodded his head. Mr. Andrus loaded up his bicycle in the pickup, and they headed toward John's house. Mr. Andrus told him he had been very polite in thanking Mrs. Andrus for the meal. He smiled at John and told him he could come eat with them anytime. John's mind was on Bob, but when Mr. Andrus told him he could eat with them anytime, he smiled and remembered Mrs. Andrus' cherry pie and black-eyed peas. It took his mind off Bob. Mr. Andrus continued talking to him about how Mrs. Andrus always cooked something for each of the three meals of the day. John asked him what she was cooking the next day. Mr. Andrus smiled and said, "Cherry pie, for one thing." John asked him if he could come eat with them. Mr. Andrus looked at him and said, "We'll see you at lunch."

They arrived at John's house. Mr. Andrus took the bicycle out of the truck. John was moving it to the storage shed when he walked past his mother, who was working in the yard.

"You're home early," she said. "What happened?"

"Ike got in trouble and then on the way home I busted my chain and Mr. Andrus brought me home," Ike replied as he continued to the storage shed.

John's mother looked at Mr. Andrus, who was standing in front of his truck.

John put his bike in the shed and walked into the house through the back door. He thought about Bob and how scared he had been. But Mr. Andrus had taken care of everything, and it was over.

He went to the living room and glanced out the front picture window. He noticed his mother and Mr. Andrus talking, and she had her hands on each side of her face like she did when she received bad news, or if she was excited about something. Eventually she grabbed Mr. Andrus's big right hand with both of her hands and looked him in the eye. She was intently saying something to him. Then she came in the house. She saw John and bent down on her knees, looked at him, and then hugged him. She continued to hug him and then told him she loved him.

She said, "Are you hungry? I've got some apple fried pies."

"Yes ma'am," John replied. If there was anything that could come close to Mrs. Andrus' cherry pie, it was his mother's apple fried pies.

She hugged him hard again and for a long time.

John always knew his mother loved him, but she had been over the top since he came home today. He could only guess that Mr. Andrus had been complimenting him and telling her that John was someone who was responsible. He figured his mother was happy because John had been listening to her when she talked about what kind of person he should be. Yeah, he decided, it must be that he was responsible. All in all, it had been a pretty good—maybe even very good—day indeed.

THE DAIRY FARMER

Travis Knight was sitting on the back of a flatbed 1956 one-ton Ford truck watching Louis Long, a local dairy farmer and Travis's employer, call his cows into the milking barn. Travis looked on with curiosity as Mr. Long would walk out of the barn, look at the fifty head of cattle eating hay outside the barn, and then call the names of three cows. He did it only once and three cows would come out of the scattered, meandering herd to the barn. They would go in and get in place for Louis to hook them up to the milking machine. Travis was fascinated by this one act. It was effective and efficient. He only wished the "meat on the hoof cattle" he was raising with his father were as smart as Mr. Long's dairy cattle. He had concluded that maybe other than sheep, cows were the dumbest animals on the planet. Even with his dog's help, he had a hard time taking control of cattle, moving them into the pen, and then getting them to do what he wanted them to do, even if it was for their own benefit.

Travis had called Mr. Long earlier in the summer to ask him for a hay hauling job. He had a threefold purpose for wanting to work. He didn't want to hang around his parents' farm all summer and let his dad think of things for him to do. His dad paid him sometimes, but it wasn't the same as having a real job, like a lot of his friends at school. Secondly, he wanted to make his own money and add to his allowance. He wanted to have his money to spend on things that were important to him. His allowance was mostly for food and clothes. If he wanted to play pool at McClain's Grocery, he needed to have enough money to put a quarter in one slot for the pay-to-play pool table. The other player had to supply the other quarter. The third reason he wanted to work was the most important. He was going to play high school football. He knew that, as a freshman, he wouldn't be on the varsity team; he needed another way to make an impression. Two-a-days were going to be tough. They were always in August when the Texas heat was its worst. He had never participated in two-a-days. He played junior high football and had been touted as varsity quarterback material. He wanted to show he was just as tough as the rest of the ninth graders. To Travis, toughness was on top of the list. At five feet eight inches tall and about 105 pounds, he looked skinny. He could make up for his slight appearance by being tough.

He also wanted other people to recognize his masculinity, especially girls. He felt like working hard in the hay fields would give him muscle strength and endurance. He was getting the impression that girls and boys his age were thinking he was an egghead, nerd, and all-around weird guy. He had excelled in athletics, but he had done even better in academics. He was valedictorian of his eighth-grade class. He always knew the answers to teachers' questions, and his mother insisted that he dress nicely when he went to school. He was beginning to think he was all by himself. None of his so-called friends asked him to do things with them anymore, and they told him they were busy when he asked them to do something with him. He thought he was doing everything right, but he knew something was wrong. He got the impression that his successes were bothering people his age. If he could show them that he was tough and a great athlete, it would go better for him.

Mr. Long came out of the barn and approached Travis. Travis set the paperback book he had been reading, "Where The Red Fern Grows", on the truck bed. Mr. Long was a thin man, not much bigger than Travis. He wore jeans and rubber boots along with a long-sleeved cotton shirt. He sidled up to the back of the flatbed, put his arm on the wooden bed, and looked at Travis.

"Hot, ain't it Travis?" Mr. Long said as he tongued a toothpick around the front of his mouth. He had probably just eaten. Mr. Long ate twice a day. Once after milking at 4:00 am and again before milking at 4:00 pm. In the summer, he cut, raked, and bailed hay in between milkings. He had two daughters who sometimes helped him, Sophia who was two years older than Travis and Bobbie Jayne who was about the same age as Travis. Both knew how to milk cows and how to cut and rake hay, but only Mr. Long ran the baler. It was a complicated piece of machinery that scooped up the cut grass with rake-like tongs. The grass was transferred into a chamber where a hydraulic system compacted the hay and then pushed it out to a station which wrapped each small square bale with hay rope. Then the bale would fall on the ground. It was the hay hauling crew's job to pick up the bales on the ground, put them on the flatbed truck, take them to the barn, and stack them in a manner that used the space most efficiently. There also had to be easy access to the hay. Mr. Long needed enough hay to feed his dairy cattle all year around, but especially for the winter.

"Yes sir, it's hot," answered Travis.

Mr. Long looked to the west and said, "I got Dub Martin coming today to help you. There are about four hundred bales sitting on the ground over in that pasture east of here on Smith Hill Road. Bobbie Jayne will drive the truck while you're in the field. You'll have to drive it from the field to the barn. I don't want Bobbie Jayne driving that full load on Smith Hill Road. She's not strong enough to handle that loaded truck out there with traffic."

"Just me and Dub?" asked Travis.

"Yeah, I can't find anybody to work these days. I shure am glad I have you. One of you can stack and the other one can load."

Travis had seen Sophia and Bobbie Jayne helping him milk. He knew Mr. Long couldn't find enough workers to help him, mainly because he didn't pay enough. Most commercial hay haulers charged ten cents a bale to haul the bales from field to barn and then stack them, although Travis had heard it had gone up to twelve cents with some haulers. The breakdown of payment with commercial haulers was forty percent for the driver and truck and sixty percent for the crew. Mr. Long used the same formula. He got four cents for each bale because he had the truck and the driver, Bobbie Jayne. Then he and Dub would split the other six cents. It would take some extra work to get the job done, and Travis calculated they would be working until about nine at night. They might even have to use the truck lights to haul the last load.

Travis often wondered if Bobbie Jayne actually got paid. He figured it was more like an allowance, where you worked on the family farm and the allowance was your payment. He and Bobbie Jayne had gone to school together since first grade in 1959. Now both were fourteen. She had always been pretty, but it seemed like she was prettier every time Travis saw her. He had started working in June and now it was August. At first, some older guys were working with him, and they would drive the truck to the barn. Travis noticed that Bobbie Jayne would scoot across the seat next to the passenger door while they went to the barn and came back to the field. She would talk to the guy driving, but it was minimal. All of them tried to flirt with her but she expertly ignored it. Travis knew better than to flirt with her. In the first place, he was not that interested in girls, secondly his mother would kill him, thirdly Mr. Long would kill him after his mother had him in the grave, and finally he was just plain scared of her. He had watched her over the years grow more confident about what she wanted and didn't want. He didn't like the way she acted toward other people sometime, but he knew better than to mess with her.

Bobbie Jayne wore shorts, a cropped shirt that showed her midriff, and white Keds.. She really had nice legs, Travis thought, and her breasts were getting bigger every time he saw her. Lately, especially when he started driving the truck from the field to the barn and back, the shorts seemed to be shorter and the midriff showing a little more. Travis had noticed. He had never paid a lot of attention to girls, but the desire had grown since spring of this year. It was all he could do not to look at her legs. They were just on the other side of the stick shift of the old truck. He would take it out of granny gear and put it in first to take the load out of the field. Her legs were on the other side in the line of sight. He could shift through the other gears without looking, but granny gear was so close to first he had to look at the stick. The legs in all their tan, smooth, soft finery were on the other side, and he had to stare. Something wonderful, but troubling, was stirring in him.

He talked to Bobbie Jayne just like he did at school. It wasn't much, but he didn't want to be rude. His mother encouraged him to be nice to all people and to speak to them. It gave them a sense of worth to know you were acknowledging them. Bobbie Jayne seemed to like him talking to her. She smiled and occasionally she would cross those legs. He told her something funny about his dog, Whitey, one time, and it made her giggle.

Bobbie Jayne asked, "Why did you name him Whitey?"

Travis answered, "Because he's white."

The giggle became a hearty laugh and she said, "Travis, you are so funny."

Travis didn't think it was that funny, but he appreciated her saying it. Each time they got back in the truck she would sit a little closer to him, and they would continue talking. Travis was getting tired from the work, but their conversations energized him. Dub was slowing down, but not Travis. When they got back in the truck to go to the field, it was getting dark. They would have to use the truck lights to pick up the last load. Dub was in his usual position on the flatbed, lying down to get some rest. This time, Bobbie Jayne got in on the driver's side, and Travis asked her if she was going to drive to the field.

As she got on the running board, she looked down at Travis, batted her eyes, and said in a whispered voice, "I just wanted to get in on this side so that I wouldn't have to scoot over so far."

Travis gulped. When he got in the truck to drive, there wasn't much room for him. Her legs were straddling the stick shift. He didn't know if he would be able to shift without touching her. His mind was getting fuzzy. He liked her attention, but he was going down a road he had never been on. He put it in first and as the truck picked up speed, he shifted in a downstroke to second and his hand touched her leg. She didn't move it. He moved the shift over and down for third and his hand touched her other leg. She didn't move it. He knew he should take his hand off the stick, but her leg felt wonderful. He finally pulled his hand off, and they were silent all the way to the field. Right before he pulled up to the final rows of bales, Bobbie Jayne put her hand on his thigh and kept it there. He already had an erection, but he thought his penis was going to come out of his jeans. He put the truck in neutral and slid out of the seat. Bobbie Jayne moved over to the driver's seat and smiled at him as he looked back at her. She put the truck in granny gear and started down the rows of bales.

Dub could not keep up with Travis. Travis was throwing the bales on the bed faster than he could stack them.

Dub said, "Slow down, Travis, I can't keep up. In fact, let's take a breather. Where the hell are you getting so much energy? You on drugs or something?"

Something, Travis thought. "Okay, five minutes. It's getting too dark. We need to get finished. Bobbie Jayne, stop the truck!" said Travis.

She stopped the truck, opened the door and stood on the running board. "What's the matter?" asked Bobbie Jayne.

"Dub needs a break. Let's take five minutes, "responded Travis.

Bobbie Jayne sat back down in the driver's seat. Travis sat on a hay bale as Dub lay on his back looking at the sky. The full moon was quite evident tonight.

"You know, I'd like to go to the moon with those astronauts," said Dub. "I think that would be the coolest thing.".

"Well, maybe you can, Dub. Become a pilot, get a college degree in science, and apply for it. It may take some time, but who knows?" said Travis.

"Nah, that's for people like you, Travis. You're smart. I can't make anything but Bs and Cs, and I don't have enough money to go to college," Dub responded.

Travis looked down and didn't know what to say.

After a few minutes, Dub said, "Hey, but thanks for thinking I could do it. I don't get a lot of encouragement from anybody. That's why I like to work with you. Anyway, I'm rested now. Let's get this done."

They got the truck loaded with all the remaining hay. Travis got in to drive and noticed Bobbie Jayne was sitting even closer to the driver's seat. Travis's hands touched her legs every time he shifted, and after he got it in third gear, Bobbie Jayne put her hand on his thigh. It stayed there until they got to the barn.

Travis always did the stacking in the barn. In fact, Mr. Long insisted on it. He liked the orderly way that Travis placed the bales, making them easy to pick up and take anywhere. Dub was throwing them off the truck but was about worn out. Travis kept waiting on him. After Dub had half the bales off the truck, he said, "I can't pick up another bale."

Travis started to get up on the truck, when he heard Bobbie Jayne say, "Can I help?"

Both Travis and Dub looked at her. They had never seen her pick up one bale of hay. She looked back at them and said, "Okay, boys, just because I drive the truck doesn't mean I can't handle a hay bale. In fact, Dub you can go home. Travis and I will finish."

Dub rolled off the truck bed and stumbled toward his car. Travis watched as Bobbie Jayne stepped up on the running board and got on the bed of the truck. She actually picked up a bale, set it down on the back edge of the truck bed, and rolled it off to the ground. Travis picked it up, and they kept up this rhythm until they finished thirty minutes later. Bobbie Jayne got back in the truck and parked it in front of the barn. Travis took off his gloves and went to the faucet, washed all the hay dust off his hands and face, and dried them on a small towel he always brought with him. Bobbie Jayne did the same and asked if she could use his towel. He handed it to her. She used it and then held it out for him to take. He grabbed it and she wouldn't let go. He stumbled forward and she took a step forward. Travis was one inch away from her face. She leaned forward, kissed him on the lips, and put her arms around him just above his waist. She kept kissing him, pressing her mouth against his mouth, and then she slipped her tongue in his mouth. He started kissing her back and then put his arms around her. She then moved her hips toward his groin and started moving around it with pressure from her hips. Travis thought this was great, but intuitively he knew it was going too far. He had never kissed a girl like this and certainly had never been this close to one. He pushed back on her shoulders gently and looked at her. He said, "I-I-I think we should probably stop."

"Why?" said Bobbie Jayne. "Don't you like it? I know you like me."

"Yes, I do like you, and I do like what we're doing, Bobbie Jayne. It's just that I think this may be enough for tonight." This left the possibility of doing it again sometime hanging in the air.

"I guess you're right." Stepping back from him, she smiled and said, "You're not like other boys, Travis. That's why I like you. You're considerate and sweet. I look forward to next time." With that, she walked toward the back door of the Long house. Travis followed a distance behind her and continued on to the front door. When Mrs. Long answered his knock, he asked if he could use the phone to call his daddy to come pick him up.

Travis went home and filled his plate with a 16-ounce T bone, wedge salad that was more French dressing than lettuce and a double helping of fries. Plus, two apple turnovers for dessert. As he lay in bed a short time later, hoping to go to sleep, he thought about the magnificent feeling he had when he held Bobbie Jayne. His ideas about girls had completely changed. He didn't feel like he was alone in the world, and there was a person who really did like him. His young weary muscles finally needed a rest, and he didn't wake up until nine the next morning.

He hauled hay for Mr. Long two more times before football two-a-days started. Each time, Bobbie Jayne, depending on the proximity of the rest of the crew, made it a point to get close to him. At the end of the hay hauling, he and Bobbie Jayne found a way for them to have some time alone and do some heavy kissing either standing up or sitting on a hay bale. They didn't want to do anything else, because both were close to clueless about what came next, and they were too afraid to explore it.

He had definitely made the right decision about getting tough for two-a-days by hauling hay in the summer. He outlasted everyone on the football field, including the upperclassmen. He was definitely way ahead of his classmates. However, it concerned him that one or two had quit after the first day. After the first week, eight had quit. Now there were not enough players to have a junior varsity. It appeared that he would suit up with the varsity. He wasn't sure how that was going to work out. By the time two-a-days were over and school had started, there were only five guys left on the team—he and John Black in the freshman class, and Dub and two other sophomores.

Not long after school started, Travis saw Bobbie Jayne at lunch. She was sitting next to a senior guy, Larry Miller, and had her eyes on him, laughing at his jokes. Travis walked right in front of them, and she didn't even acknowledge him. Travis thought it was weird and rude. Then it happened again, right after lunch, in English class. He walked into the class and spotted Bobbie Jayne sitting at a desk with four other girls sitting around her, giggling and talking. Travis never even got a side glance from Bobbie Jayne. After the class was over, he made it a point to walk next to her and say, "Hi, Bobbie Jayne."

She looked at him, smiled, and said, "Hi, Travis."

Travis responded, "It's great to see you. How have you been doing?"

"Oh, I'm good. I've got to hurry and get to algebra class on time. Mr. Walker can be grouchy if I'm late."

She walked away from him quickly, and Travis went to his vocational agricultural class. After all those kissing sessions, he thought he would get a little more attention from her. He still didn't understand girls.

Two days later, the head coach called him and John Black into the teacher's lounge for a meeting. He was pretty sure he wasn't in trouble, but John was nervous. The head coach told them that many of the guys who quit two-a-days wanted to come back and play. He told Travis and John there would be no junior varsity team if they didn't come back, and Travis and John would not get much playing time on varsity. However, he wanted to get their opinion on whether or not they should come back. Travis was a little skeptical, but he wanted playing time. John was okay with it. In the end, the head coach said he would let them come back.

The next day the wayward junior varsity guys came out on the field. As they went through agility drills, half of them were puking on the sidelines. John Black came over to Travis and said, "That'll teach them to skip two-a-days." Travis watched as he sized up his teammates. They were not giving him much confidence the team would have a winning season.

Late Friday, Mr. Long called to ask Travis if he could haul hay the next day. His parents had nothing planned for him, so he agreed to do it. As he hung up the phone, he wondered if Bobbie Jayne would be driving the truck. To his surprise, when he got to the hay field, he saw Sophia in the driver's seat. Dub was there and another new guy named Clint was there. Travis walked up to Sophia and asked her if she was driving.

"Yes, Travis. Who do you think did this driving before Bobbie Jayne?" Sophia laughed.

"Sorry, Sophia, this is just my first summer, and I was used to her doing it all the time," Travis explained.

"Well, she told Daddy she was sick, but I think she's faking it and waiting for a phone call from her new senior boyfriend, Larry Miller."

"Oh, okay." He replied, not trying to sound too dejected. "Well, I guess we can get started."

Travis and Clint picked up, and Dub stacked bales on the truck. It went pretty fast with three guys. Sophia didn't need Travis to drive the truck to the barn, and he rode on the back with Dub and Clint. Travis was quiet. He had been thinking about having another make out session with Bobbie Jayne ever since Mr. Long called him.

On the last load, Sophia asked Travis to sit in the cab with her. After she got the truck going down the road, she asked, "How do you like being a freshman and playing junior varsity football."

Travis responded, "It's all right, I guess. I don't think our team is too good."

"Yeah, well don't fret, I don't think the varsity team is much better. Being a cheerleader, it's hard to keep cheering when we keep losing."

For him to have a junior girl take this much time to just sit and talk to him was unbelievable. He thought she was a goddess, definitely better looking than Bobbie Jayne and her shorts were just as short. But her breasts were magnificent. She caught him staring at her and smiled back at him.

"Did you take any vacation trips this summer?" Sophia asked.

"Yeah, we went to see my uncle and aunt in Harlingen, Texas and then went across the border into Mexico at Matamoros."

"Oh, that sounds cool, I'd like to go to Mexico." Once again, she smiled at him.

"Bobbie Jayne told me you were a good kisser," Sophia said with glee in her voice.

Travis turned red from his neck through the crown of his head. Sophia looked at him and giggled.

"Don't get embarrassed, Travis. It's a nice trait to have. I wish my boyfriend was a good kisser. She also told me you were a gentleman. There's a lot to be said for having that kind of character."

After a silence, Travis said, "Thanks, Sophia. I guess I'm a little awkward around girls, but my mother has always told me to treat girls with respect."

Sophia looked at him contemplatively. "You're a good person, Travis. Keep being one in high school. It will pay off."

She pulled into the barn. By the time Travis stacked the last bale next to the roof in the barn, it was five in the afternoon. Mr. Long came over from the dairy barn and paid all of them in cash. Dub and Clint left. Mr. Long walked to the house with Travis.

"Well, that was a short one today, Travis," Mr. Long said, moving the toothpick around in his mouth.

"Yes, sir," Travis responded.

"How do you like working with my daughters?"

Oh shit, Travis thought. *Did Bobbie Jayne tell him?*

"I-I-I like working with your daughters."

"Yeah, those girls of mine are like their mama. They pretty much get their way and won't take no for an answer. They're good girls, and they sure seem to like you. Be careful around them, Travis. I wouldn't want them to get on the wrong side of you and you get on the wrong side of them. It may cause me to have to get involved."

"Yes, sir, Mr. Long. I'll stay on my side."

Louis Long laughed and slapped his knee. Then he said, "Travis, I sure do like you. You're a good worker and you treat people right. Keep doing it, son. You'll go a long way with that attitude."

Football season was horrible. The junior varsity lost every game. The varsity lost all of them except one. Some of the same guys who quit two-a-days quit again. Travis was discouraged. He had looked forward to football in high school, but the season was rotten because most of the guys didn't have their heart in it. It was chaotic on the field. Travis was the quarterback. He would call the play and most of the linemen would push and not block their assigned defensive player. The running backs would run everywhere like they were playing keep-away on the playground. They never ran the called play. Travis could count the number of first downs for the season on both hands. Forget passing. He would take the snap, pedal back to get in the pocket, and as soon as he took three steps, he was tackled. By the end of the season, he had spent considerable time on the bottom of dogpiles filled with at least four defenders. Discouraging was the best word to describe his first year of high school football.

His favorite sport, basketball, was next on the agenda. They had a pretty good eighth-grade basketball team. He thought this would be a reasonably good year. Some of the football quitters came out for basketball. Travis played point guard and soon had a starting position. Some sophomores and juniors also played junior varsity. Travis had a good shot and could score points. but his coach told him he was starting too low on his body with his shot. He told him to bring it above his head and do a jump shot to avoid getting it blocked. Travis started practicing on it, but the necessary mechanisms were like relearning his shot. But he just kept practicing and tried not to get too discouraged.

When basketball season was underway, though, it was déjà vu all over again. No one did what the coach taught them in practice. They got stomped in every game. Travis was still scoring points but it was never enough. It was also more difficult with his new jump shot. However, something else began to trouble him. He was becoming more estranged from the guys on the team and his friends in school. He talked to them, but they didn't seem to want much to do with him. Then the locker rigging started. He would open his locker and all the books would fall out. Every time it happened, he would look up and see a few of his so-called friends snickering as they watched him pick up his books. He finally got wise and opened the locker slowly, holding his hand close to the door and catching the single-stacked books before they fell. They continued to rig the locker, though, and would double-stack the books.

Then the name calling started. In the background, he could hear many of these same guys say "Kitty." Occasionally they would say "Kitty, Kitty, Kitty." He would look at them, and they would laugh hysterically as they walked away from him. He didn't get it. Some of these guys he had known since first grade. He had never experienced being ostracized from his own friends. Most of them had been the two-a-day quitters. He tried to ignore it, but he didn't look forward to coming to school. Basketball was terrible and now this stuff. All of these jokers were older than he was. There was no one taking up for him and siding with him.

Physical bullying started next. He would walk around a corner and a couple of them would be waiting for him. They would push him, then trip him, and his books would fall when he lost his balance. He would get back up and go into class. In class, he would hear the low voice, "Kitty, Kitty, Kitty." He started looking around every corner before he walked around it. Even then, they started getting bolder. They were always in twos or threes. One would push him and one or two of them would hit him in the back or on the head and then run away. He didn't know what to do. One on one he would take them on, but two or three of them was too much.

One day, Sophia was walking toward him when it happened again. Before they could run away, she said, "You stupid jerks. Leave him alone. Why don't you pick on someone like me? I'll take you on and whip all your scrawny asses." Then she kicked Kevin Stephens in the butt. "And you should know better, Kevin Stephens. I'm going to tell your mama." All those guys looked afraid, even though they were the same size as Sophia. She helped him pick up his books. Travis didn't say anything. He couldn't look up because a couple of tears were rolling down his cheeks.

Sophia said, "Travis, look at me."

Travis shook his head.

"Travis, look at me," she said once again in a stern voice.

Travis looked at her because he didn't want to lose what looked like the only friend he had in school. Sophia saw the tears.

"The best way to defeat bullies is to bloody their nose. By that I mean, you pick the one who is doing the most bullying. Then you take it to him, every ounce of you. You fight to win. Don't worry about the consequences. You haven't done anything wrong. They are just jealous of you. You're such a great student, a good athlete and a great person. They can't stand it. They're jealous of you. They want you to be more like them. These guys are jerks and probably always will be. Kevin Stephens is my cousin. His mother is my dad's sister, but she is married to a jerk, and Kevin acts just like him. His dad is a mean small-minded piece of garbage and couldn't hold a light to my dad or your dad."

"Thanks, Sophia. I-I-I could use a friend," Travis answered as he stood a little taller now.

"Anytime," she replied. Then she took a step toward him, kissed him on the cheek, and walked off.

Travis was regaining his confidence. He never thought a girl older than he would be as nice to him as Sophia had been. She had just affirmed everything his parents had been telling him and more. He strode proudly into his all-boys health class, not at all bothered by a substantial number of them saying "Kitty, Kitty, Kitty" as he entered the classroom. Kevin Stephens was in the back of the room. Travis sat in the front.

Mrs. Tolar, the school nurse, taught the class every spring. She was a good teacher and kept reasonable control of her class. However, on this day, every time she turned her back to the students and went to the chalkboard, pea gravel started to fly from the back of the room. Travis took a few hits and picked up the small rocks. He kept hearing "Kitty, Kitty, Kitty," and he knew he had to make a move right then and there. He stood and aimed one straight at Kevin's forehead. It hit him right between the eyes, which went wide with surprise. Travis smiled and sat back down. A moment passed and Kevin walked up to Travis's desk and pushed his books onto the floor.

Travis came out of the desk and tackled Kevin. The hay hauling and sports conditioning all came together. Using both hands, he landed a flurry of punches while Kevin was on the floor. Kevin tried to get up, and Travis tackled him again. He kept hitting him in the face with his left hand and punching his balls with his right. He wanted to hurt this guy badly. All the other boys were standing back cheering them on. Finally, Mrs. Tolar dragged Travis off Kevin.

Kevin jumped up and looked around. He seemed scared. This was the second time today he had lost status with the other boys. Questioning looks abounded among the boys as they stared at Kevin. He then started yelling, "You hit me in the balls. I'm going to make you regret it."

Mrs. Tolar told Kevin to go to the principal's office and then gently guided Travis out the door. She gave the other boys an assignment and quickly caught up to Kevin, who was trying to be menacing but not getting very far with Travis. He was two years older, thirty pounds heavier and four inches taller, having failed twice to advance to the next grade.

Kevin had played with Travis when they were younger, and they had been at each other's houses on numerous occasions. That had not happened in the last three years. Kevin had looked down on Travis because he was younger. But now, Travis knew the real reason. Travis just ruined his bullying status. He was ready to take him on again. In a fair fight, Kevin didn't have his sycophants with him.

Mr. Morris, the principal, heard the story from Mrs. Tolar. He then talked to the boys about it. Kevin was sullen. Travis was giving Mr. Morris his rapt attention. He told them there was to be no fighting at school. He was going to give each of them four licks from the paddle. Kevin went first. Mr. Morris told him to go back to class. Travis was next. This was the first time he had gotten licks in school. Mr. Morris definitely went lighter on him than he did Kevin.

Then Mr. Morris looked at him and said, "Travis, I heard from Mr. Long you were having some problems with bullying. Sophia and Bobbie Jayne told him. He came to me. I'm going to have a conference with your parents, and I'll figure out a way to get this stopped. Right now, I'm glad you are taking some action on your own." He winked at him and told him to go back to class.

As Travis entered the classroom, all heads were down working on an assignment. Travis walked up to Mrs. Tolar, and she quietly explained the assignment. He went to his desk and noticed all his books were stacked neatly on it. He put them in the storage area under the desk and started working on his assignment. The lunch bell rang, and Travis headed for the cafeteria. As usual, since the end of football season, he sat by himself. When he sat down, he saw Sophia and her boyfriend, Jim, along with some other girls in the junior class. Sophia looked at him and smiled. He smiled back at her. He then opened the novel he was reading, "Exodus", and began eating his lunch.

He was concentrating on the book and his food when he sensed someone was standing next to him. It was Thomas Aldrich, a junior who got picked on because he just did some weird thing, like looking off into space when he talked with his sonorous voice and big lips. Travis didn't know him very well, but he didn't like what the kids and some of the teachers did to him.

Thomas looked at Travis with a hangdog stare and said, "I heard you just whipped the shit out of Kevin Stephens."

"Well, yeah, we got in a fight, and I was the last one on top."

"Thanks," said Thomas and awkwardly offered his hand for a handshake. Then he turned around and walked away.

As Thomas walked off, Travis noticed Sophia getting out of her chair and moving toward him. She stopped about a foot in front of him, smiled, and said, "Hey, Travis, would you like to come sit with us?"

Travis looked over where she had been sitting and noticed all the girls looking at him, but not Jim. Travis didn't care. He was pumped up and could use some friends.

"Yes," Travis responded. He got up and sat down across from Sophia and next to Linda Taylor and Jane Tanner. He was in the midst of the best-looking girls in high school.

Linda smiled and asked, "Travis, are you going to the prom?"

"No, I'm just a freshman," Travis answered.

"Well, you could go with a junior or senior girl," responded Jane.

Travis and Jim looked at her with questioning expressions and Jane said, "Well my boyfriend is a sophomore, and he's coming with me."

Travis said, "Well, I like to dance and would like to go to the prom, but my mother would probably say no because she would want to know all the details of the girl who was taking me, her family history and the family history of everyone else at the prom."

All of them laughed and then Sophia said with a smile, "I think there are a lot of junior and senior girls who would like to be your prom date. Do you have a girlfriend, Travis?"

Jim was staring hard at Sophia. "No," Travis said as he looked into Sophia's eyes.

Linda and Jane giggled as Sophia and Travis kept looking at each other. The conversation then turned to more lighthearted stories, and Travis laughed with other people his age for the first time in a long time.

Spring came with its beauty. Wind blew in the warmth, and rain watered the East Texas landscape. Travis started spending a lot more time outside. He was running track and competing in the half-mile race.

The track coach approached him one day and said, "Travis, I think you can be a good half-miler if you watch, Waymon. Even though he was a sophomore, he made it to the regional track meet last year and placed second. Watch him and his technique."

Thanks, coach. I will," Travis answered.

By the time he had run his first competitive race, Travis was staying close to Waymon. After the race, Waymon saw Travis and said, "Hey, Knight, good race."

"Thanks, Waymon, I just barely placed sixth, though," Travis answered.

"Man, you're just a freshman. That's good. You keep pushing me and keep those other guys from gaining on me." Waymon then slapped him on the back.

Travis smiled. For the first time, Travis felt like he was doing something right in athletics. By the time the track team got to the district meet, Waymon had won first every time and Travis was gradually moving up to third and fourth place finishes.

The bullying gradually went away. After his fight with Kevin Stephens, his locker no longer got rigged. He had one more confrontation, this time with Darold "Shotgun" Welch, who called him "Kitty."

Travis looked at him and said, "What did you call me, Misfire?" Travis knew that Shotgun did not like to be called "Misfire".

Shotgun pushed Travis in the chest and Travis pushed him back, and they ended up wrestling on the ground.

Travis was on top when Mr. Morris broke up the fight. He took them to the office, lectured them about fighting, and gave them four licks with the paddle. As Travis was leaving, Mr. Morris winked at him. It was the last bullying incident for Travis.

Apparently, after Mr. Morris's visit with Mr. Long, Mr. Morris had taken an active approach to what the high school boys were doing to Travis. He told Travis's dad that they were like organized crime. One would hang around and see where Travis was going and signal to the others. They would hide and attack Travis when he came around the corner. They tried it a few times after the fight with Kevin, but Mr. Morris caught them, took them to the office, and gave them licks. He told them if he caught them doing it again, they were going to get double the number of licks. Travis felt free. He still didn't have friends, but he was happy. He was looking forward to summer.

There was one thing Travis was sure of. He was not going to stay in this community after high school. He read enough books, saw different places in person and talked to other people to know it was not his destiny in life. Just three more years, and he would be gone. He wanted to have the money to buy himself a car and go to college. He needed to stay in shape for athletics. The solution was obvious: go back to work in the hay field.

The first week out of school, Travis was already working for Mr. Long. Bobbie Jayne was driving the truck again this summer. She had evidently broken up with her senior boyfriend. She began sitting close to Travis in the cab of the truck, and they resumed some of their make out sessions after the hay was in the barn. It never went any further than kissing. Bobbie Jayne made that clear with Travis, and he was fine with it.

When the middle of July came around, Travis's dad told him about a friend who needed a rod man for a survey crew. It paid much more than he was making in the hay field, and Travis jumped at the chance. He told Mr. Long and then Bobbie Jayne that he had another job. Mr. Long wished him well and thanked him for the good work he had done. He gave Travis a new pair of work gloves and a baseball cap. Bobbie Jayne caught him in the barn and kissed him for a while. She told him she would miss him.

The new job was good as far as the pay. He also learned a lot, even if it was a little boring. And there was a guy on his crew named Rodney who started picking on him, somewhat like what he had experienced at school. Travis was about to confront him when Rodney suddenly left the job.

Relieved to be rid of Rodney and more eager than ever to achieve his financial goals, Travis told his dad he wanted to keep working, even through two-a-days. He would rather have the money than put up with quitters and slackers on the football team. There was a new coach. His dad went to him and explained Travis's need to make the money. The coach somewhat understood but told Travis's dad that his playing time would be limited. Travis thought it was okay. He knew there would not be enough players for a junior varsity, and he wouldn't get to play very much varsity anyhow.

With his bank account substantially filled, Travis walked on to the football team on the first day of school. He was in good shape from working and had no difficulty staying up with the rest of the team. The other players were already griping and complaining about the coach. Some had quit. Their starting quarterback was a sophomore who was one of the quitters last year. He broke his collarbone before they played the first game.

The second quarterback had played with Travis in the eighth grade. He was a decent athlete, but he didn't even play his freshman year. Now he was the starting quarterback. Travis suspected it wouldn't last. Sure enough, by the time they had played the second game, he had broken his wrist.

Neither one of these guys were in good condition, and their toughness had always been questionable. The coach had initially put Travis at tight end. He was mostly blocking on offense, and playing in the secondary on defense. He ultimately became the third starting quarterback and remained in that position through the rest of the season.

Twenty-eight boys suited up for the first game. By the last game, they had fourteen. The other fourteen were injured or quit or failing their academic classes. They lost all their games except one. It was a 0-0 tie.

The football coach was also their basketball and track coach. They lost every game. But Travis kept going and wouldn't quit. He ran track. He told the coach he wanted to run the half-mile. The coach refused to let him. Forced to run the mile instead, he did all right and even placed once. But he hated the mile race.

More importantly, Travis was not bullied the entire year. He did not get into one fight. He was beginning to be as tall and as filled out as most boys his age and even some boys older than him. They knew he would fight them and left him alone.

He was in Spanish class with two new guys who had transferred from Houston schools, Kent Edwards and Ray Allen. One day, Travis bumped Kent with his desk and turned to look at him. Travis said, "Sorry."

Kent answered, "Hey, no problem. What's your name?"

"Travis." Travis offered his hand to Kent. Kent shook it and then introduced Ray to him.

"Ray and I live next to each other on Sullivan Loop. We just moved here."

"Yeah, I know. I heard both of you came from Houston."

"Yeah," Ray said. "Hey, you probably know your way around here. Why don't you hang around with us this Friday night when we go to town. We need to get educated on the culture around here, man, and especially the girls."

They all laughed and then Travis said, "I don't have a car or a driver's license."

Kent said, "I have both. When can we pick you up?"

Travis was elated. However, he feared his parents may nix this get together. He looked at Kent and said, "I-I really want to go, but I-I need to check with my parents."

Kent smiled, "Sure, man. I get it." He wrote down his phone number and gave it to Travis. "Call me tonight and let me know if you can go. How about we pick you up at 6:00 pm, and we can get a hamburger?"

Soon they were spending a lot of time together. Travis was happy. Even if everything in sports was horrible, at least he had some friends. He also started winning awards for his academics and his speaking abilities. He was admitted to the honor society as a freshman and by his sophomore year, he led his class in grades.

Unlike Bobbie Jayne, who had moved on and started dating a guy from the nearby town of Lum, Travis had only one date his entire sophomore year. A girl from Lum asked him to the band banquet. She and Travis had the same music teacher, and they had played in recitals together. Travis didn't know what to do when she asked him and told her he would have to check and see if he could go. He talked to his mother, and she seemed to be excited about it. He was nervous, but his mother helped him through the whole experience. Three couples went together in a huge Chevrolet sedan with a bench seat. Travis liked it. His date was very pretty and so were the other girls. Travis had a good time. He didn't kiss his date, but he enjoyed sitting close to her and also dancing with her. She smelled like the roses his mother grew in their yard and the slow dancing was as good, if not better, than the make out sessions with Bobbie Jayne. Her entire body was moving with him and getting him aroused to the point of wanting to hold her even closer. She didn't seem to mind.

When school let out for the summer, a man Travis's father knew asked Travis to work for him at his air conditioning business. Travis jumped at the chance. He was supposed to clean up the shop and keep things organized. The owner told him he would teach him how to fix window-unit air conditioners. Travis kept the shop very clean and organized all the work spots so that the workers could do their work easily.

He was getting paid $10 each day for eight hours of work. The first week he got his $50 check. It was the most money he had ever made in a week. The second week he got a $40 check. He told the owner there had been a mistake. He only got $40 this week instead of $50 like he received the first week. The owner said it was no mistake. He told Travis he hadn't shown enough initiative in fixing the window unit air conditioner. Travis was speechless. The owner had never shown him how to fix them.

On Saturday, he called Mr. Long and asked him if he had any hay to haul. Mr. Long said he was doing his big field on Monday and could use him. Travis told his dad he was going back to work for Mr. Long after what the air conditioning owner had done to him over his wages. His dad was angry with the owner and told Travis he was going to call him. He encouraged Travis to go ahead and work for Mr. Long. He said Travis learned a good lesson about working and earning money—always work for people who are going to be honest and straightforward with you.

When Travis got to the hay field, Sophia was driving the truck. She seemed a little distant and wasn't quite as friendly with him as she had been in school. She had just graduated. Travis thought she would be doing something else besides driving the truck. They exchanged pleasantries and then got to work. Two guys he had never seen worked with him. They didn't know much about hauling hay, and Travis had to instruct them on the best ways to handle each bale. He had to load and stack. He never thought he would be a hay hauler instructor. They finished around four, and Mr. Long paid them.

Mr. Long looked at Travis and said, "Travis, I do believe you are getting taller and are putting on muscle there, boy."

"Yes, sir. I'm five feet nine inches tall and weigh 140 pounds," Travis answered.

"Well, boy. You're almost as big as me. You keeping those thugs at school under control?"

"Yes, sir. They don't bother me anymore."

"Good. It looks like they better not try!"

Travis laughed, "Yeah, Mr. Long. Hauling hay for you and working on our cattle ranch-- fixing fence, feeding and doctoring cattle and branding calves-- keeps me in pretty good condition. I don't put up with a lot of nonsense."

"You just keep it up. Travis, when you are smart and successful, people like to drag you down to their level. They are jealous. It's one of the sordid things of human nature. And they'll keep doing it unless you stop them. Don't put up with bullies."

Mr. Long had a smile on his face and a gleam in his eye. Then he said, "I'm going to keep an eye on you. I know you'll be one of those people who help our community, this state, and the whole nation. You've got what it takes to make a difference."

Travis smiled at him, noticing that he was the same height as Mr. Long. It was good to hear these words from someone besides his parents and teachers. He said goodbye to him and got on his bicycle to ride home. It was still daylight. He headed to the rice canal for a swim. Just a few people knew about the huge water well that pumped groundwater into a canal next to the Scott rice field. The water was used to keep the rice submerged during the growing season. It was cold and just the thing to do after a hot day of hay hauling.

He parked and found a place to take off his sweaty hay hauling clothes and change into a pair of cutoffs he had brought along. He walked into the water. It was bracing but felt extremely good. One reason people didn't know about the rice canal was the grove of pin oaks, sweetgums, and willow trees that surrounded it. Travis couldn't see out toward the road, but he could hear cars and trucks passing. Today, there was no traffic.

After he had been in the water for about ten minutes, he heard a truck approaching and coming to a stop. He was disappointed. Now he would have to share it with other people. Then he heard giggles and talking from what sounded like two girls, and quickly recognized Bobbie Jayne and Sophia's voices. He grinned and thought it would be interesting to swim with them. They appeared at the edge of the water and Sophia announced, "Travis Knight, you've got company."

Travis replied, "Come on in. It's nice and cold."

He noticed that Sophia was still wearing the shorts and shirt she had been wearing when they worked earlier in the day. Bobbie Jayne was wearing something similar. He didn't see either of them holding a bathing suit. He waited for them to go back to the truck, get their suits, and change behind the trees. But that's not what happened. They both started taking off their shirts and then their shorts right there in front of him.

Travis was frozen. He had never seen a girl in her bra and panties. Now he was seeing two of them. Then Sophia looked at him and smiled, and then looked at Bobbie Jayne, who gave her a short nod. Both girls gradually took off their bras and then slowly took off their panties. Travis couldn't close his eyes. They were stunning. It was perhaps the most beautiful thing he had ever seen. Both girls were giggling as they walked into the water and toward him. The water just covered their naked breasts and Travis didn't know what to do as they watched him in their advance toward him.

Sophia spoke first, "All right, Travis. Show us."

Travis was speechless. What was she talking about? He still could not take his eyes off them.

"Okay, Travis," Bobbie Jayne said, "We took off our clothes, now you have to take off yours!"

Oh God. Travis thought. *I'll get in serious trouble if my parents and Mr. and Mrs. Long find out.*

"Now, Travis, Sophia said, looking stern., "Get up on that bank and take off your cutoffs."

Travis remembered when Sophia got mad and kicked Kevin Stephens in the butt. He didn't want her to do it to him. He got up on the bank, took off his cutoffs, and stood naked before them. They started giggling again. Then he looked at his penis. It was about one inch long, shrunk because of the cold water. He started turning red.

Bobbie Jayne said, "Come on in, Travis. You're such a sweet boy and I think you look handsome in all your naked glory."

Sophia replied, "I agree."

Travis jumped in, splashing them hard, and then they got into a water fight. They all laughed, swam, dove off the bank, and had a great time, enjoying the cold water in the hot sun for about an hour. Then the girls said they had to go home. They got out, put their clothes on, said goodbye to Travis and went home. Travis marveled at what had just happened to him. He would never forget it.

That day turned out to be the last time he would haul hay for Mr. Long. The next day, he applied for a high-paying position working on the highway that ran in front of his house, and he got the job. He also got his driver's license that summer, so he could drive himself to work. And he had his first date on his own with a girl named Angela Barrett. It was a real treat because Angela was so much fun and full of life. He had a good time with her. But Travis was not interested in just one girl. There were a lot of them he would like to get to know better. He tried to date Bobbie Jayne, but she turned him down twice, and he never tried again.

One evening when he was in town, he saw Sophia at the Dairy Queen. She was sitting by herself. He walked up to her and said hello. She had a half smile for him and asked him to sit down. She didn't say anything, but Travis knew she was disturbed about something. Her hand was on the table, and he put his hand on it. He said, "Are you okay, Sophia?"

She looked at him and shook her head. "No," she said as a couple of tears came down her cheeks, "I just broke up with Jim and it was kind of hard to do."

Travis didn't know what to say to her. He just held her hand. Then Sophia looked out the window and asked, "Is that your new car out there?"

She was looking at his 1963 Ford Galaxy 500.

"Yes."

"You haven't asked me to go riding in it yet."

"Let's go," Travis responded. He took her by the hand and opened the passenger side door for her.

Travis got in the driver's seat and asked her, "Where do you want to go?"

"The hay field."

Travis looked at her curiously, then put the car in gear and drove to the Long hay field, where the hay had just received its second cutting. He parked in the middle of the field. It was getting dark. The full moon was coming up in the east and the stars were everywhere.

They sat there and looked at the moon. Sophia slid across the seat and got next to Travis.

She said, "There were plenty of times I wanted to sit next to you in the seat of that hay truck. But I was going with Jim, and I didn't think I should be doing it. He gave me a promise ring, and I was trying to honor it. The trouble is that he wasn't doing the same thing. I knew he had been going out with other girls before the day we came to the rice canal. I didn't care if you saw me naked because I knew you would respect me. I still think that about you, Travis. You respect everybody."

She leaned into him and kissed him on the lips. He put his arms around her and held her close. They kissed for a while. They sat and watched the moon as it rose in the sky.

"What are you going to do, Sophia?" Travis asked.

"I'm a high school graduate. I've always wanted to be a journalist because I like to write. I thought I was going to marry Jim, but now I'm glad I got the freedom to go pursue that dream."

"I think you would be a great journalist. You are honest, articulate, and you know how to tell a good story. You are also very beautiful. You'd probably do well on television."

She reached up, turned his head, and kissed him passionately. Then she took his hand and put it on her breast. He felt it gently and thought it was the most magical thing he had ever touched. In a few moments, she slowed things down, moved his hand away from her breast, and looked out the window again.

"Thanks for spending this time with me, Travis. You are not just a sweet boy. You are a real man. Some girl is going to be lucky to marry you."

Travis was a little confused. *She was kissing him. Wouldn't it be possible for them to be married one day?*

As if she could read that thought, Sophia said, "You're too smart for the girls in this community. They know it. I know it. There are things you are going to do that we would never be able to understand about you or support you. It's something inside we all feel about you. It's scary and wonderful. I'm just glad I got to know you."

Football and basketball were much better the next year. The team had a new head coach. He worked them hard. He demanded that they be tough or get off the team. Some did. The team didn't win a lot of games, but they were competitive. The football team was small but had a reputation for being hard-hitting and never quitting. They ran a straight T triple option offense. Travis was one of the team's leading rushers as quarterback.

The next year, Travis's senior year, the football team won the district championship and went to the state playoff quarterfinals. Travis was their second leading ground gainer. Because his team ran the triple option and because Travis was valedictorian of his class, the University of Texas offered him a football scholarship. He didn't play much during those college years, but the scholarship gave needed financial assistance for a college education. In 1975, he got a business degree. He was extremely interested in the burgeoning business of computer and information technology.

Forty years after his time with Sophia in the hay field, Travis stood looking at the coffin of Louis Long. He had just read Paul Harvey's short essay "So God Made a Farmer" at the graveside service. He reminisced about hauling hay for Mr. Long and the simple wisdom he had passed on to him. He thought about how Mr. Long had made it a point to back up his parents and help him with bullies at school. He also had passed that moral fiber along to his children. He watched them as they sat with their families. All of them had come back to this community to raise their families and to pass on that same heritage of good character and caring for other people.

Travis, in his career as a computer software business entrepreneur, had been among the first to bring the revolution in information technology to Texas. His development of the computer and computer software industry infrastructure around the Austin area was legendary. Politicians curried his favor, and he was peerless when it came to respect among his business partners and competitors. He had become a billionaire. His influence and standing were well known throughout the world. He was considered a tough, honest businessman with a lot of compassion. His employees loved working for him.

He had kept in touch with Mr. and Mrs. Long, Sophia, and Bobbie Jayne. Sophia would call him about once a year and tell him how they were doing. She had become a journalist, but decided her family was more important than her career. She had been married for thirty-two years and had three children. She occasionally wrote for some magazines. One year, she told Travis that her dad was having a hard time with his old baler and would not buy a new one. He didn't want to make those big round bales like everyone else and was having a hard time finding parts for the old baler. Travis asked one of his vice-presidents of procurement to research the problem and find the best baler to replace Mr. Long's current one. When he got the information, Travis called the dealer, bought the baler personally, and asked them to deliver it to the Long address with a note that the baler was for Louis Long from an admirer. Sophia called him after the delivery and told him she knew it was him. She was crying while she was talking to him. He listened to her. When she paused, he said, "Sophia, your family gave me much more than what that baler is worth. You gave me your love. It was priceless."

After the service, with Travis's wife standing by him, Bobbie Jayne and Sophia came to him and both of them had a twinkle in their eyes when they hugged him. Many years ago, he had realized what they had taught him about love between a man and woman. It was also priceless. He had been married for twenty-eight years to the same woman. They had two children. Sophia walked with him out of the cemetery as Travis's wife walked to their car.

Sophia said, "Travis, do you remember that night in the hay field?"

Travis looked at her and responded, "Every minute of it."

Sophia looked at his wife as she walked to the car. Then she said, "Isn't love grand? Does she take good care of you?"

Travis smiled as they looked in each other's eyes and then answered, "Yes, she does, Sophia. In her own way, she kicks my bullies in the ass."

They laughed heartily as she put her arm in his arm, and they walked out of the cemetery.

ACKNOWLEDGEMENTS

Gratitude is the best word I can give to my wife, Susan Rice, my sister, Mary Martha Barnett, and my daughter Faith Rice-Mills for taking the time to read these stories and encouraging me to publish them.

My editor, Mary Summerall, gives me direct and thoughtful advice, which I take seriously. My proofreader, Leo Bricker, polishes each story.

And many thanks goes to Melissa Burch and Alex Burch for letting readers know this book is available for them to read and enjoy.

Most of all, I appreciate those who read my stories.

ABOUT THE AUTHOR

J. Andrew Rice was the founder of Public Management, Inc. and was its CEO for thirty-three years. He also has other business interests. He has a bachelor's degree from Baylor University and a master's degree from the University of Houston at Clear Lake City. He serves as a deacon of Rural Shade Baptist Church and was its Minister of Music for thirty years.

He has four children, four grandchildren, and lives with his wife in Tarkington, Texas. His hobbies include music, reading and farming.

He is the author of the novel, *Seeds of Bliss*.

DISCOVER MORE ABOUT J. RICE'S WORK

For more information about my work, upcoming projects, and exclusive content, please visit my website at www.jandrewrice.com.

Thank you for joining me on this journey. Your support and feedback mean the world to me. If you enjoyed this book, I would greatly appreciate it if you could take a moment to leave a review on Amazon. Your thoughts and reviews help other readers discover new books and support the creative efforts of authors like me.

Thank you once again for your support, and I hope you continue to enjoy my stories.

Made in the USA
Monee, IL
15 September 2025

25725716R00049